BYE, SWEETHEART!

DHANUSHKUMAR P

I would like to dedicate this novel to all the video games
that inspired me to be creative enough to create
something new.

Contents

Contents

Acknowledgements

As I take this moment to reflect on the journey of publishing my novel, I feel it is essential to acknowledge the incredible support I have received from those around me. First and foremost, I would like to extend my heartfelt gratitude to my professors. Their guidance and encouragement throughout my studies have been essential in developing my understanding of storytelling and the art of writing. The thoughtful feedback and steadfast support they provided were crucial in bringing this novel to life.

Next, to my parents, I am deeply grateful for your infinite love, unwavering faith in me, and the consistent support that has carried me through this journey. Finally, to my friends, your companionship and encouragement have fuelled my inspiration and motivation. I especially want to thank Nikita and Ranjitha, whose proofreading skills have greatly enhanced the clarity and precision of my manuscript. Your keen eye for detail means a lot to me.

Lastly, I am profoundly thankful to Prakalya, whose expertise, thoughtful suggestions, and editing skills took this novel to heights I could not have reached on my own. Their dedication and commitment to excellence are truly valued.

Also, I would like to express my sincere gratitude to the creators and developers of "**Mafia: Definitive Edition**." The game's compelling narrative, atmospheric world-building, and richly developed characters served as a significant source of inspiration for my novel, 'Bye, Sweetheart!'. While my novel is a unique work of fiction, the impact of "Mafia: Definitive Edition" on its creation is undeniable, and I am deeply appreciative of the inspiration it provided.

Prologue

It was an unusual day in the central Ruby, with usual traffic and pollution. It was a summer day. The sun was shining as it had been the previous day and people were rushing with their cars on the road to get to their offices. The blaring horns of cars were deafening, a typical Monday in 1990.

I parked my car in front of the cafe and entered. I ordered a strong black coffee and looked out at the nearby police station through the windows of the cafe. I finished my coffee and started eating the cookies. The waitress asked me if I wanted a refill, and I accepted. I waited for some time, enjoying the view and the fresh air.

Precisely at 10:30 AM, I left the cafe and got into my car. I drove into the police station parking lot. It was my first time visiting a police station, and it was a new experience. I entered the police station building and excited as well. At the entrance, a middle-aged lady was sitting behind the bars with the door open. She saw me and asked, "Sir, what do you want? Do you want to file a complaint?" In an inaudible voice, I replied, "No ma'am. I want to meet Detective Angelina." She didn't understand what I said, so she asked, "What?" I repeated, "Detective Angelina. I want to meet Detective Angelina."

Still unable to hear me clearly, she requested, "Sir, please come near the bar so that I can hear you properly." Following her request, I moved closer to the bar and repeated, "Detective Angelina. I want to meet Detective Angelina." She was a little confused and shocked, and questioned me about Angelina. She asked, "Hey, man? How do you know about her? She just received her transfer letter yesterday. How do you come to know about her? Anyways, she will be here in 15 minutes. Why do you want to meet her?" I replied, "I want to..." [She stopped me]. She asked me to fill out the visitor form and handed me a pen. Then she asked me, "Are you able to write, or do you need help?" I said, "No, ma'am, I can write on my own. Thank you."

While filling out the form, she said, "You looks familiar, but I am not able to recollect my memories." I smiled at her and handed over the form. She checked the form and froze in shock. She took her gun and shouted, "Ethan, Ethan is here." The fellow policemen on that floor also aimed their guns at me. One of the policemen pushed me down and checked my pants and shirt pockets. I was handcuffed by the same guy who pushed me to the floor.

Yes, I knew. I created a mess at the very beginning of the week. The reception lady called Angelina and informed her about the situation. The reception lady kept saying yes to Angelina on the telephone. After she hung up, she called the headquarters and asked for reinforcement. Lieutenant Benjamin of the Central Ruby Police Station was on the second floor, and she asked a few men to carry me up to the second floor. They locked me in a corner cell. Lieutenant Benjamin called the policemen on the ground floor using the intercom and asked them to lock the main entrance and to be alert. Then, he asked them to open the door to policemen who had proper ID. If anyone else tried to open the door, he gave orders to shoot them down without damaging the door. The policemen were still aiming their guns at me, even though I wasn't carrying any arms. Lieutenant Benjamin radioed headquarters to ask them to block the street with an armed vehicle and requested helicopter support.

There was a newly recruited police officer who was clueless about me, asking nearby policemen about me and the reason I was locked in that cell. I noticed him inquiring about me to his senior officers, who were busy aiming their Glocks at me.

Everyone's faces were filled with fear, which was new to me because I was at the cell of police station. The cell was lit by a small bulb, and there were six cells on that floor. Every prisoner was staring at me, some of them knew me, while others were clueless like the new police officer. I was still handcuffed and felt thirsty. I wanted to be uncuffed because it was uncomfortable and my shoulders began to feel pain. So, I said, "Hey buddy, I'm not carrying any weapons and I'm 78 years old. Could you please uncuff me? It's hurting. Also, I'm thirsty, so could you give me some water please?"

Lieutenant Benjamin said, "You tricky bastard. You killed 167 police officers in your life, and now you're asking for water in a police station?" I was shocked by the number because hadn't counted the number of cops I had killed. It was surprising that these officers had a record of my kills.

Suddenly, the intercom rang. Lieutenant Benjamin picked up the call and listened to the person on the line, then gave an order for the person to open the door before ending the call. After a few minutes, a young woman with a ponytail came to the second floor and found me. She walked over to me, standing in front of me with steam coming out of her ears. However, I was safe behind the Iron grill gate, which protected me from her wrath. She reminded me of Abigail and I couldn't turn my eyes away from her. Her eyes, like those of my love, were sharp, with small ears. Within few seconds our eyes were locked, I could see her urge to kill me in her eyes.

She then moved to a nearby table and sat down, shouting, "At ease, this old shit will no longer be a threat."

Everyone on the floor holstered their guns, and she grabbed a water bottle and drank it before asking for my files.

The old policeman on the floor went to the third floor to fetch my files, leaving me filled with unnamed emotions. I continued to stare into her eyes, but she eventually noticed and to break the tension, I asked for some water. She signalled to a man next to her to give me a water bottle, but he hesitated, questioning why they should give water to someone who had been a nightmare for the Rubians. But she once again gestured him to give me a bottle and said, "He will suffer pain in prison, not now." Then he brought me a full bottle of water.

I grabbed the bottle and sat in the corner of the cell. Then I opened the bottle and drank it fully. After drinking the water, I began to stare at her. Then, my memory began to recollect everything. My happiness, my sorrow, my rewards, my love, my struggles. Everything was coming before my eyes.

Suddenly, the intercom began to ring again. Lieutenant Benjamin picked up the call and nodded three times. Then he ended the call. He pointed out two men and asked them to help the men on the third floor. As he gave the order, the two policemen went to the 3rd floor.

Then Angelina asked one of the policemen to bring the register to her. A few minutes later, the policeman brought the register. She opened it and took a pen from the pen stand near the monitor. Then she signed it and placed the pen back in its place.

Then I heard footsteps above my head. I thought it was the sound made by the men on the third floor. After a few minutes, the men from the third floor climbed down to the second floor. They were carrying six heavy boxes and placed them near Angelina. She was shocked and opened one of the boxes. One of the three men said, "Ma'am, these are all the case files related to the Mechanic gang. Initially, we did not have these files. However, three years ago, during the renovation of all police stations, they were handed over to our station. If we hand over Ethan to the court, we also have to hand over these files."

Angelina was shocked to see the six boxes. I think she was stressed, and may have thought that my case would be a burden for her. The three policemen returned to their work after handing over the files to her. She opened one of the boxes and took out one of the files. Then she began to glance through my file. I watched every move Captain Angelina made. She had the courage to do difficult tasks. She had been on the second floor for the past 13 minutes. Perhaps.

I asked a policeman standing near me for the time. At first, he ignored me. But after several attempts, he raised his right arm to check the time. He said, "It's 11:32." I thanked him and asked for his name. He pointed to his name badge, and I read it. His name was Harrison Ford, which reminded me of the Hollywood actor. Out of curiosity, I tried to ask him about his name, but he was not willing to discuss it. He said, "Shut the fuck up, asshole."

It was very silent, like a night in a graveyard. Every man on the floor was watching me without even breathing, except Angelina. But the silence was not lost. Suddenly, the telephone rang near Lieutenant Benjamin. Everyone jumped in fear at the sudden ringing sound. Even Angelina gave a little jerk, which made me giggle. Then she stood and went to pick up the phone. She answered, "Captain Angelina Thomas," and listened to the person on the line. I didn't know what was happening on the call, but I was sure it was not happy news or information to her.

She ended the call by saying, "Okay, Sir." As I thought, it was a news that did not bring her joy. Benjamin asked what happened on the call and who was on the line. Angelina replied, "It was the chief of police. He wanted us to keep this bastard secure until the escort team arrived. They will come by 5:00 PM. They are planning for a special court hearing for him. In the meantime, he is going to send a news reporter to record audio about Ethan's life. I think probably the judge will sentence him to death instead of hanging him like a dog."

After hearing this, everyone was frustrated to have me on the floor. Even Angelina was not happy to have me on the floor. She might see me as a pain for her. Then she radioed to inquire about the position of guards on the floor and in the parking lot. Angelina came near me and said, "See, there are just five and a half hours left. So, cooperate with us. Be on your Best behaviour. If not, you know what will happen." Then she sat on the chair where she had been sitting before.

Everyone began to take a breath. Some of them started to do their regular work in the police station. Some of them were still in fear, but soon this fear was lost on me and everyone began to treat me as a common accused.

Like a kid who watches his mother working in the household, I watched the people working there. I wasn't able to sit for a long time because of my back pain, so I lay on the table but I didn't stop staring at Angelina.

Time passed, but I didn't stop staring at her. After a few minutes, she offered me a hamburger. I wasn't feeling hungry, but I took the hamburger from her hands without hesitation. I unwrapped it and took a bite. It was delicious. I ate the whole hamburger and kept the hamburger wrapper in my pocket.

Every man on the floor mocked me for keeping the wrapper, but I didn't pay them any mind. Suddenly, the telephone rang. Angelina picked up the phone and answered the call. It was a short conversation. I didn't know who was on the other end of the line. She informed the other men, "The news reporter will arrive shortly, so make room for him. Clear the tables near Ethan."

As she ordered, everything was arranged. The computer and table were lifted and replaced within a few minutes. Once again, the intercom rang. This time, Benjamin answered the call and got the information from the person on the line. Then he hung up and informed everyone, including Angelina, that the reporter was arrived and was expected to reach this floor in a few seconds.

As he said, the reporter arrived shortly and introduced himself to Angelina as Richard Jones. Then he approached me and introduced himself, and I did the same. He placed his large bag on the nearby table and began to unpack everything. He set up some stands and mounted the camera. Upon seeing the camera, Angelina became tense and started to argue with Richard, but the situation was resolved peacefully after Richard showed her the permission letter signed by the chief of police and permitted him to capture video.

Richard then continued to setup. After completing his work, he asked Angelina to place the microphone inside the cell where I was locked. She willingly assisted him, holding the mic in one hand and a gun in the other. Harrison opened the cell gate, then placed a table in front of me and left the cell while aiming his pistol. Once Harrison had exited, Angelina entered, placed the mic on the table, and locked the cell before leaving.

Everyone on the floor paused their work to watch us. They made space for themselves to have a clear view. I felt like an actor on a stage. At that moment, the fearsome creature became an entertainer. I suspected that Angelina would not scold them for neglecting their work.

Richard made some tuning work on the camera and asked me to say hello to clear the audio clarity. I said "Hello" and he replied, "Thank you, sir. It's clear. Have some water and make yourself relax and comfortable, then, we can start our interview." I replied "I'm okay." Richard smiled at me and said, "Let's start our interview, Sir."

CHAPTER ONE

A ROUGH START

I was born in Texas on November 4, 1912. Richard Woods and Mary Woods are my parents. My father worked on a ranch near our house. However, I was never sure of its exact location. Many of my childhood memories have faded over time. My mother was a talented cook and pianist, and she also worked as a nanny for our neighbor's babies. I spent my early years in Texas until the age of six, then we moved to Moonshine Town.

In Moonshine, we resided in the 8th house on Abraham Street, across from the Sunset Bar. The bar owner's son was my childhood friend, although I cannot recall his name now. When we moved to Abraham Street, my father struggled to find a job, and we often went to bed hungry. Thankfully, a man named Martin the Master helped my father secure a job, allowing us to live comfortably.

As time passed, my mother also began working as a cook, and I became the apple of my parents' eyes. I relished the joy of my childhood, but it was short-lived. When I was 12 years old, my mother tragically died in a fire at her workplace. I was devastated by the loss, unable to fully grasp the absence of my beloved mother. My father too was left feeling lost and alone after she passed away.

She was a beautiful woman with her childlike smile. She was the soul of my family. But she was gone. Due to the loss of my mother, my father became a drug addict. He stopped going to work and began selling all the things in the house to buy drugs. The house was empty, like my heart. A few weeks after my mother's death, my father hanged himself in his room. Then I became an orphan.

I roamed around my street for a few days. Some helped me with their food, and some kicked me away. Fortunately, Master Martin came to know about my situation. He picked me up from the street and gave me some cookies. Then he asked me to get into his car. He gave me courage and promised me that he was there for me. The car stopped in front of a house where a man seemed to be eagerly waiting for someone. Master got out of the car and extended his hand to help me out. I walked to the house holding his hand. Then he made me sit on the sofa while he sat at the dining table. They were talking, but I didn't know what they were discussing.

There was a dog with a name tag on its collar. Its name was Bruce. While they were in conversation, I spent time with Bruce and enjoyed it. He was a pet dog. But I didn't know that I would spend my entire youth in that house with Bruce.

As Martin's men exited the house, Master Martin came to me, kissed my cheek, and said, "Take care, my son" before leaving the house. Then the two people came near to me and sat next to me on the sofa. They introduced themselves to me. He was Ben James and she was Margaret. They were husband and wife. They made me comfortable and both kissed me on my cheeks. They played with me the entire day and at night, they showed me a separate room for me to sleep. I didn't spend a single day alone, but I didn't say anything. I just entered the room and said, "Thanks." She said, "From now on, it's your room and your space. From now on I'm your mom, and he's your dad. Okay, sweetheart?" In hesitation, I said, "Okay, Mom and Dad." They felt happy to hear me addressing them like that. She gave me a strong kiss on my cheeks and said, "Good night, honey." I replied to them with good night. They exited my room by closing the door slowly.

It was a nice room with a window, a bed, and some boxes. I wasn't curious about the boxes but about the window. It gave me a nice view of a lake which was reflecting the moon. It looked like the soul of my late mother. The moon reminded me of the beauty of my mother. That night, I didn't sleep until the moon disappeared. I was awakened by my new mother with kisses. She was trying to make me feel comfortable and to forget the loss of my parents. She did the same partially.

When I woke up, Bruce was licking my toes, which made me giggle. I brushed my teeth and descended the stairs where my mom was preparing breakfast. She noticed me and asked me to go to the backyard, where my father was busy with his work, and requested me to fetch him for breakfast. I ran to the backyard and Bruce followed me. As I reached the backyard, I saw a car garage where my dad was working. There were three cars in the garage, and my dad was repairing the engine of one of them. Bruce barked as we approached, catching my dad's attention. He smiled at me and gestured me to come closer. I ran to him, and he asked, "What's the matter, young man?" I replied, "Mom called you for breakfast." He stood up, cleaned the grease off his hands at the nearby tap, and joined me for breakfast.

We entered the dining area where my mom had already set the table. She instructed me to sit down, and my dad sat next to me. Mom served breakfast with a smile on her face. It was a delicious meal that I will never forget. Mom also served Bruce's breakfast in his bowl as he sat on the floor next to me. That day was unforgettable because I once again felt safe and comfortable after my loss.

CHAPTER TWO

AN UNBROKEN CIRCLE

We finished our breakfast, and then I went to the garage with Bruce because I loved that place. The garage was had three cars, and I gently touched every nook and corner of these cars. Then, I sat in the driver's seat and imitated driving. I love cars. I used to watch cars roaming here and there from my old house, but unfortunately, I wasn't able to get into a car before. It was my first time being in a car. I sat in all three cars, but I liked the red-colored car, while others were in milky white and ocean blue.

It was a very gorgeous car, and I didn't know that this car was going to be a part of my entire life. Then, I heard my mom calling me. I ran to her, and she held my hands and we went outside of the house. We waited in front of the house for dad to come. Suddenly, I heard a rapid thundering sound coming from the backyard, getting closer to us. Finally, it was the red car. I was shocked to see the car that had captured my attention. I was so excited to board the car, and my mom helped me get into the back seat. However, my dad insisted me to come and occupy the front seat next to him. My heart was filled with excitement and happiness as he started the car and began to drive.

Then my dad stopped the car in front of a clothing store. My mom held my shoulder from behind and said that they were going to purchase clothes for me because I didn't have a spare dress to wear. I felt like the happiest person in the world.

My mom and dad began to browse through each and every dress in the store. They chose many dresses and then brought their selections to me, asking me to choose the ones I liked. I replied, "I like everything." Without hesitation, they said, "Okay." They then asked me to try on one of the dresses in the fitting room. As instructed, I changed into it. My mom took my old dress from my hands, held my hand, and we walked out of the store, where she tossed my old dress into a nearby garbage bin.

We walked to a nearby restaurant that looked good and smelled of tasty food. We sat at a table in the corner. As we sat down, the waiter approached us and took our order. I don't recall exactly what we ordered, but it tasted good. After finishing our lunch, we left the restaurant and crossed the street to get back to the car. Just like in the morning, I sat in the front seat. My dad smiled at me, started the car, and after a few minutes, it started to rain, but we didn't get wet. I loved the entire day. When we arrived home, my dad opened the door for me. I jumped out of the car and ran into the house.

That night, I wasn't able to sleep because of the excitement that was created by the red car. My mind was filled with images of the car. I didn't even consider the wonderful dinner prepared by my mom, the dresses my dad had bought for me, or the goodnight kisses from my mom, as I was completely focused on the red car. Eventually, I fell asleep.

The next morning, my mom woke me up with lovely kisses. I quickly brushed my teeth and hurried to find my dad. My mom informed me that he was in the garage, so I rushed over with our dog, Bruce, following me. When I reached my dad, he greeted me with a smile on his face. I asked him if I could drive his car, but he just laughed. I asked again, and this time he grabbed me and sat me in the driver's seat. After closing the bonnet, he sat in the front passenger seat next to me. He pointed out the accelerator, clutch, and gear shifter, and said that he would teach me how to drive after breakfast. I was insisted him to teach me immediately, but he managed to convince me to wait until we finish our breakfast. It was, as always, a delicious meal.

I finished my breakfast very quickly and waited for my dad to finish his plate. After he washed his hands, I dragged him to the garage and asked him to begin the teaching. He appreciated my interest and began to instruct me without starting the car. When he completed his instruction, he asked me to start the engine, but I forgot the instructions he had given me. So, he taught me again and made me start the car. Then he instructed me to move the car forward, which is out from the garage. As he instructed, I drove the car.

CHAPTER THREE

A BROTHERHOOD

I started getting adapted to the new place and accepted Ben James and Margaret as my new parents. They didn't make me feel like an adopted son; instead, they treated me as their son. Their house became a home for me. It was on Heaven Street, but now it is changed to Peter Street. It was a huge house compared to the houses in the neighbourhood, with extra space for a garden, backyard, and garage compared to my old house.

Master Martin and his family lived on Church Street, which was a street hidden from mine. Master Martin had two sons, the elder one named Samuel Jackson, whom we call Sam, and the younger one named Daniel Rich, whom we call Danny. One day, Master Martin visited our home for dinner with his family, including his wife, Sandra, and his two sons. While they were engaged in a lively conversation in the dining room, Sam, Danny, Bruce and I went to the garage and played. That was the day I met these people, and soon we became brothers. Sam is a year elder than me, while Danny is one year younger than me.

We used to play together in my garage and in the backyard of Master's Villa. Some days, I sneak into my parent's room to steal the car key after he slept in the night. I used to pick up Sam and Danny at Uncle George's Restaurant, which is near their house, and drive them to Alligator Lake, which is behind the church-on-Church Street. We used to throw stones into the lake to provoke the alligators in it. Many times, we were chased by alligators, but as we had a car, we managed to escape. It was very fun to do that. Danny used to stop running when chased by an alligator and would cry loudly instead of running.

All our adventures went smoothly until the day that completely cut off our adventure. I can remember that day as if it happened yesterday. As part of our routine, we decided to go to the alligator lake and provoke some silly alligators. However, we could not find the car in my dad's garage. So, we decided to walk to the alligator lake. Danny was crying out of fear and said that he was not coming with us. We tried to convince him, but he was very stubborn. Therefore, we went to the lake without Danny.

It was very calm out on the lake. At first, we stood near the lake for a while to enjoy the calmness. Then I picked up some stones and gave a few of them to Sam but he refused to take the stone. I was clueless at that time and asked him, "What? What is the matter?" He replied, "It's boring." I asked him, "What's boring? Be specific." He said, "The stones. How many days are we going to throw stones at the stupid alligators? It doesn't feel like the first day. It's boring." I asked him, "Then what will we throw at them?" He pulled out six dynamites from his pockets. At first, I didn't know what it was. I asked him, "What is this?" He said, "It's explosives. I took them from my dad's car boot when he was in a meeting in the house." It was clear that he brought the dynamites to throw at the sleeping alligators. I said, "Wait. Do you know what will happen if our parents find out? It's night. This place is very quiet. It will create a huge explosion sound and wake up all the people in the surrounding areas. So don't be foolish. Put the explosives back where you found them." But he was not ready to listen to me. He said, "No, it will not make such a loud sound. It will sound like a firecracker. So don't panic and take it." I believed him and took them from his hands. He gave me three dynamite sticks and kept the remaining three with him. He also brought some rope to tie them together. He tied his dynamites first, and then I tied mine.

Sam gave me a lighter, and he had one as well. We both opened the brass lid of the lighter and spun the flint wheel at the same time. The lighters began to light. Sam asked me to follow his count. He said, "When I say one, we should light the fuse. When I say two, we should aim at the alligators, and when I say three, we should throw them to the alligators. Okay? Are you clear?" "Yes, Sam, I am clear," I replied.

I did as per Sam's instructions. When he said three, we threw the dynamites at the same time towards the alligator's head. It blasted with a huge explosion sound and threw us away from the lake. We did not get hurt, but we somehow managed to get up. When we opened our eyes, nearly all the houses had switched their lights on, and some people came out of their houses to check the explosion. We were afraid to face our parents, so we decided to escape sight undetected by the people around us.

We tried our best to run to our houses, but some people saw us escaping from them. Fortunately, they did not see our faces due to the lack of light. Sam's house was closer to the lake than mine. So, we decided to run to his house.

Finally, we reached his house. We used a ladder to get into Sam's room. First, Sam climbed up and knocked on the window to wake up Danny to unlock it. Danny unlocked the window, and we both entered his room. Then we took a deep breath and felt relief.

Danny nagged us to explain what happened and what the explosion sound was. At first, we hesitated to tell him, but eventually, Sam revealed everything that had occurred. Danny was shocked and stated, "Daddy went to the explosion site with his men, and he knew that the explosions were caused by his explosives." We were stunned, and Sam asked, "How did he know that the explosions were created by his explosives?" Danny replied, "Who else in this town has explosives other than our father? It is very obvious." We were very afraid to face Master Martin. Suddenly, we heard footsteps on the stairs, and we were nearly paralyzed with fear. Then we heard a knocking sound on the door, and a voice calling for Sam and Danny. It was Master Martin. We were silently crying in the corner of the room, facing the door. Master repeated their names several times, and finally, he called out, "Ethan. Open the door, son." That's when I opened the door.

Master entered with Aunt Sandra. He instructed Aunt Sandra to leave the room, and she complied. Master sat on the floor and asked us to join him. I went first and sat down next to him, while Sam and Danny were initially fearful of their father but eventually sat down as well.

Master reached into his long coat pocket, pulled out some cookies, and offered them to us, encouraging us to eat. As we began to nibble the cookies, which were prepared by Aunt Sandra. He asked, "Who did this?" Danny revealed our involvement. Master glanced at us and remarked, "That was wrong. You killed six alligators and damaged the church. Killing unnecessarily will make us pay for it. You are kids, but you have responsibilities. After me, you are going to take care of this town. I killed many, but not unnecessarily, so be like the kids and enjoy your childhood. And you, Sam, don't try to steal anymore. Okay?" We nodded our heads and he said, "Alright, you guys promised me to be on your best behavior. So, follow the promise. Ethan, it's already late. You stay here. Tomorrow, I will take you to your house." I nodded my head. Then we laid on the bed. Danny fell asleep first, but Sam and I slept a little bit later.

Master woke us up and took me to my home in his car. My parents were waiting outside for me. Master opened the door for me. My mom and dad ran towards me and hugged me. My dad thanked Master. Then, they walked aside and began to talk about something. Master asked my mom to take me inside, but I didn't want to go inside without knowing what they were talking about. My mom offered me a sandwich to eat, and she asked, "What happened?" But I didn't tell her anything. Soon, my dad came inside and sat next to me. He said, "Don't worry. It's all right. From tomorrow, I will teach you everything about cars, and in the evening, you can spend time with your friends." I said, "Okay, dad." And I went to my room.

CHAPTER FOUR

CARE AND KILL

Days went on. I reached 18. I was a car Mechanic at that time. My dad, Mr. Ben James, was killed in a shootout when I was 15. After his death, I found out that my father was also in the Gang of Master Martin. Even after his death, we were stable financially. But my mom was always thinking about her beloved husband. She was nine years younger than my dad but she refused to remarry. They got married in 1922, and I don't remember the exact date and month. They were in love and got married. They were a lovely couple but now she was alone.

It was November 1930. I was 18 years old. One day, while working in the garage, my mom told me she was going to the church near the lake. It was a routine for her to go to church every day after my father's death and she would return at lunchtime. After finishing my work in the garage, I took my dad's Red Ford T model car, which was my favourite car from my dad's collection. I parked the car in front of Master Martin's Villa and picked up Sam and Danny with me. It was our daily routine to drive near the mountain road in my car. We used to hunt wild rabbits and deer once or twice a month. That day, Sam shot a wild rabbit and we cooked it. We had a delicious rabbit roast with beer for lunch. Then I dropped them off at their house.

I drove back home, parked the car in the garage, and entered the house through the back door. I called my mom, but she didn't respond. I searched the dining room, storage area, and kitchen before going upstairs. Once again, I called her, but she didn't respond. I went to her room and heard a weeping sound. Slowly pushing the door open, I was shocked to find my mom crying with scratches and bruises on her hands and face. I asked about the wounds, but instead of answering, she hugged me tightly and continued crying. I tried to calm her down, but she wouldn't stop weeping. Finally, she opened up about what happened. She explained that as she was leaving the church, a group of five rogues was teasing a woman on the street and they also teased her. Out of anger, she approached them and spat on the face of a man who seemed to be the leader of the gang. In response, they tried to mistreat her. She tried to escape and some nearby people helped her fight against them, but they wouldn't leave her alone. Luckily, a police car arrived on the street, and in fear, the gang members left my mom and ran away. I felt my head begin to heat up like the sun. I asked her to describe the men in the gang, and she said they all had a green band around their foreheads.

Filled with rage, I took my mom to Master Martin's house and left her with Aunt Sandra. Without her knowledge, I brought Sam and Danny with me. I explained what had happened to them, and Sam asked me to drive to the old man's pawn shop. We entered the pawn shop together. When the old man saw us, he said, "Welcome, kiddos. The future Mechanics, come. I'll show you what you wanted." He directed us to the hidden room in the store. It was pitch dark, and I wasn't able to see my own hands. Then the old man switched on the lights. We were amazed and shocked to see the room. The room was filled with handguns, machine guns, rifles, semi-automatic guns, grenades, shotguns. The old man said, "Pick what you want, and it's free for you. Only for the first purchase." And he laughed aloud.

Sam picked a heavy machine gun, but I stopped him and asked him to choose one of the handguns. Then he chose a revolver. Danny and I chose a 1911 pistol. The old man could not stop laughing and he gave us extra magazines with loaded bullets. When we were about to leave the shop, the old man stopped us and asked us to sign the register. As he said, we signed it. Then we got into the car, but we all felt slight fear about Master Martin because we were doing this without his knowledge. But my anger made me feel like a beast seeking blood.

I drove to the church and inquired about the gang. Most of them did not know where the gang was, but some said they would be under the bridge near Railway Street. So, we went to that street and found some guys wearing green bands on their foreheads. We got out of the car. There were four of them. They saw us and walked near us. One of the green band fellows asked, "What do you want, kids? Are you guys lost from your family?" and they laughed. I said, "Some of the cock suckers in your gang teased and misbehaved with women on Church Street, including my mom. They are five. So, if you show me that fuckers, I will let you live, otherwise your brains will be on the floor." After I spoke, they began to mock us and fearlessly admitted that they were the ones who had teased my mom and other women.

This triggered and unleashed the monster within me. I grabbed the gun and shot three of them to death, turning myself into a murderer, a monster, in a matter of seconds. At that moment, I felt no worry or guilt, as I wanted them dead. When the fourth man saw the gun in my hand and it's aimed at his head, he begged for his life. I demanded to know the whereabouts of the fifth man, and he disclosed that the man was at a nearby motel called Happy Stay Motel, identifying him as Hudson. I then shot the fourth man dead and got into the car. Sam and Danny were shocked yet excited, seeming to enjoy being a part of such activities.

Upon reaching the motel, Sam and I surveyed the area while I asked Danny to check the register for a guest named Hudson and his room number. The motel appeared rundown, resembling a garbage dump. When Danny returned and informed us that Hudson was in room 7A, we searched the ground floor to no avail, as no rooms ended with letters. We then proceeded to the first floor, where all room numbers ended with the letter A. Then, finally, we found the room with the number 7A.

I knocked on the door many times, and we decided to kick near the doorknob at the same time. This time, I counted up to three. At three, we kicked the door and the lock was broken. When the door was opened, we saw a naked man and a teenage girl having sex in bed. I pointed the gun at the man, and the girl covered her naked body with the bedspread and ran away. I asked, "Are you Hudson?" He said in fear, "Yes. Wha..." The next second, I shot him in his chest, head, and stomach. I didn't stop shooting him until the rounds were over in my magazine. Sam controlled me and said, "Ethan, he is dead. Come. Let's escape before the cops arrive." Then we escaped from the place in my car. Finally, the rage and the monster within me settled down. Within a day, I killed five bastards. I didn't know at that time that killing would continue in my life.

CHAPTER FIVE

BLOODSTAIN

I drove the car to Master's House. I parked the car in his garage front and entered the house. Everybody in the house was staring at us like strangers. Then Aunt Santra interrupted us. She cried but she controlled it. She moaned, "Bloodstain. Bloodstain cannot be washed. Now it has stained your soul as well." She cried and took a deep breath. She said, "Go inside. Martin is waiting for you." As she said, we entered the room.

Master Martin and his men were sitting in chairs. It was my first time entering the Master's meeting room. He asked us to sit in the chairs. At first, we hesitated, but he forced us to take the seat. He offered us water, and we drank it. When Master asked about things that happened that day, I didn't say a single word. Then he asked Sam. Out of fear, Sam narrated the entire story of what happened that day to him. Master silently listened to everything. After Sam finished telling Master, he did not say anything, but silently thought about something. Then he had some water and began to speak.

Master asked me, "Did you know how your father, Mr. Benjamin James, died?" I replied, "He was killed. He was shot in a gang war." Master nodded his head and said, "He was like a brother to me and very loyal. He stood as a pillar for the Mechanic gang. There was a treaty signed by me and Joseph to stop the gang war between us. The treaty stopped the fights but could not quench the Cold War. So, we decided to have a car race competition. Ben James was my champion for the third year and remained champion for six consecutive years. Then he fell in love with your mother, Margaret, and married her. I told him to leave the gangster life and be a good husband and car race champion. He followed my advice. But in 1927, I was shot on the road by the Iron Gang, so, he once again picked up the Tommy for me, and as a result, he died. He wanted you to continue his legacy as a racer and did not want you to be a murderer. But now, it's all gone."

Both of his eyes were filled with tears. He wiped his eyes and drank some water. Then he continued, "I wanted to keep you away from this hell, but I failed to protect you from it. If you get a bloodstain once, it will never be washed away. These five murders have genuine intentions. You may have reasons for these murders, but you are going to kill many people without any intention or motive. You are going to kill many people as a mercenary. A kill will not stop at just one. It will ask for more. [Master took a deep breath.] Take care of yourself. Meet me tomorrow in the same room." Then he left the room quietly.

Sam, Danny, and I were clueless. We left the room. I searched for my mom, but I was not able to find her. I asked the maid about my mom. She said that Aunt Santra and my mom were in my house. So, we decided to go to my house and got into the car. As we were about to leave, a voice came from the nearby restaurant. It was Uncle George. I had known him for many years. All the dishes in his restaurant taste good. He called us to his restaurant. We got out of the car and entered his restaurant.

George welcomed us with a smile and made us sit. Then he offered us chicken fried steak with salad and milk. He sat opposite me and said, "Welcome to the Mechanic gang." We were shocked, and Sam asked, "You too are in this gang?" He replied, "Yes. Most of the people in the street are members of the Mechanic gang." We were stunned and asked him, "Why did you call us to your restaurant?" He said, "I want to tell you something as a senior member. The history of the Mechanic gang; the history of vengeance; the history of violence that has happened and is happening." We nodded our heads and said, "We're all ears."

Uncle George began to tell the history. He said, "At first, we were all in the single gang. The people called us 'The Moonshine gang', where Martin's father, Lawrence, was the leader. We dealt with weapons, ammunition, cars, and drugs. Lawrence was always in the protection of his two sons, one was Martin and the other was Joseph. Joseph is the elder brother to Martin. Martin was the favorite child of Lawrence and was very loyal to his father. However, Joseph was quite the opposite of Martin and Lawrence. Lawrence was not interested in prostitution and faced many problems with Joseph and his supporters who wanted prostitution as one of our businesses. But Lawrence did not accept Joseph's approach. So, Joseph built a brothel house outside the moonshine, without the knowledge of his father, and kidnapped many young girls from the neighboring towns. Joseph was addicted to women and stayed in his brothel house. He impregnated 17 young girls within a month. One day, a girl escaped from the brothel house and approached Lawrence for help. She told everything about Joseph and his brutal actions. Immediately, Lawrence sent his men to the brothel and asked them to kill all of Joseph's men and bring Joseph to him. By the evening, Joseph was under Lawrence's control. Joseph begged for his life, but Lawrence wanted him dead. Martin convinced his father to spare Joseph, and Lawrence let Joseph leave Moonshine. Lawrence took the women from Joseph's brothel house and sent them to their respective places, but some of them refused to go back to their native homes and asked to stay in Moonshine itself. Lawrence made arrangements for their living and medical support for those who wanted to abort their babies. Lawrence was broken because he trusted his elder son, Joseph, and believed he would be his successor. However, Joseph ruined everything.

Danny interrupted Uncle George and asked, "So Joseph is my uncle, right?" Uncle George replied, "Yes," and continued his storytelling. He mentioned that many loyal friends of Lawrence asked him to find and kill Joseph because they knew he was evil, but Lawrence refused due to Martin's request. Three weeks after Joseph's exile, a normal night at Lawrence's warehouse turned tragic. Every night at 11:30 PM, Lawrence's men would count the stocks in the warehouse, closing it by midnight with only four guards on duty. Unfortunately, the entire warehouse, including the guards, were burnt to ashes. Initially thought to be an accident, Lawrence later learned that Joseph was behind the fire. Lawrence was furious and wanted to kill his son, but Martin intervened and promised to handle Joseph himself. They began planning Joseph's demise but struggled to locate him. Despite searching every corner of Moonshine, they couldn't find him. Meanwhile, Lawrence's health deteriorated. Eventually, they discovered Joseph's hiding place. We felt happy to find the snake's hideout, but at the same time, we received information about Joseph starting his own smuggling business and gathering nearly 200 people in his gang. He smuggled Iron ore, women, and engaged in some private deals. He named his gang 'The Iron Gang'. We were ready to execute our plan as we had sketched it out. Martin prepared to hunt down his own brother. Martin went to Joseph's hideout, stealthily placed a bomb, and detonated it from a distance.

Once again, Danny interrupted Uncle George and asked, "Is Joseph dead?" This time, Uncle George became angry and scolded Danny for interrupting his flow. Then he continued his narration.

He said, "The bomb blasted. Martin went to the blast area to check for Joseph's body, but he couldn't find it. So, he returned to his house in Moonshine. The scene shook Martin to his core. Everyone was crying outside the house. Martin went inside and entered his father's room, where more than 20 gang members were mourning. He made his way to see his father. He was shocked to find Mr. Lawrence David chopped into pieces, with his fingers and eyes removed. Martin was furious at Joseph. Everyone knew Joseph was responsible for Lawrence's death, but we couldn't take further action without proper evidence. After Lawrence's death, we faced many gang wars between The Iron gang and The Moonshine gang. Some of the Moonshine gang members joined the Iron gang, some retired and settled elsewhere with their families, and some supported Martin and his gang. Joseph was very successful in the Iron ore and prostitution business, but he did not succeed in the car business. He was cheated by many in the car business. Therefore, Martin chose automobile smuggling as the key business and named the gang "MECHANICS." Martin's automobile smuggling operation was very successful, and the Mechanic gang expanded.

However, Joseph was not happy about this and started causing trouble for us, leading to a gang war.

Uncle George then asked me, "Do you know about your father?" I remained silent, and he continued to talk about my father. He mentioned that my dad, Ben, was also a member of their gang and was very loyal to Martin. Ben was their getaway man. The gang wars continued, affecting many political parties. The ruling party, The Public Union Community (PUC), stepped in to try and resolve the conflict between the Mechanics and the Iron gang. The PUC party initiated a peace treaty between the two groups. Master Martin was happy with the motive and the treaty, so he signed it willingly. However, Joseph signed it out of compulsion.

After the meeting, Joseph stopped them and proposed a racing competition to prove their superiority. Master Martin agreed to the racing competition. For the first two years, the Iron ores racer won the cup. However, in the third year, my father, Benjamin James, entered the race. He remained the champion for six consecutive years and died as the champion. After his death, the Iron gang members started winning the champion trophies for the past two years. Uncle George expressed uncertainty about what would happen after my father's death. He said, "For the past ten years, they had been at peace according to the treaty, but now they broke it."

We were shocked when Danny said, "We thought that we broke the contract." Uncle George said, "No. The Iron bitches broke the contract first. According to the contract, nobody from both gangs should create direct or indirect problems for the other gang, its members, and their families. The Iron gang broke the contract first. However, you guys also broke the contract by killing Iron Gang members. The most important issue is that the man Ethan killed in the motel is the brother-in-law of Barrett, the elder son of Joseph, who is known as 'Father'." He has two sons, Barrett, known as 'Shotgun', and Arthur Morgan, known as 'Bear' because of their appearance.

After Uncle George's story, we realized that we had fallen into a trap where blood flowed like a river and there was only one way out. We were speechless. We left Uncle George's restaurant and got in the car. We couldn't accept the truth. I drove the car slowly to my house and parked it in the garage. The garage reminded me of my dad, and I cried. Sam and Danny tried to stop me from crying, but they couldn't. I apologized to my dad, knowing it was too late. Eventually, Sam and Danny managed to stop my tears, and we entered the house through the backyard door.

Sam, Danny, and I entered the dining room where my mom and Aunt Sandra were sitting. My mom saw me and rushed to hug me. Then she started to cry and told me, "Now, your hands are stained with blood, my son. It will not be washed. Your father and I wanted you to stay away from this hell. It is not the life you deserve. This hell swallowed your father and now... I do not want to lose you, but it's too late." She cried loudly, and Aunt Sandra and I tried to console her. She knew the end of that journey, so she was ready to accept the reality.

My mom made us sit in the chairs and said, "From today, your life is in danger. From today, you will not be able to live a common man's life. Now, you are in the Mechanic gang, and it is the safest place for you in the entire world because they will protect you." But I knew that she didn't like me to be a part of the Mechanic gang. We nodded our heads and said, "Yes, mom."

Then she hugged and kissed me. I took her to her bed and made her go to sleep. Then I sent Sam and Danny to their house and went to my room. But I could not sleep; I was thinking about my future and death. I even had hallucinations that my entire body was soaked in blood. That night, I did not sleep. I recollected every single second of the day. It was horrible. But Sam and Danny enjoyed every kill of mine. That day, I came to know that Sam and Danny are of the mindset that killing a person is a pride. And I knew that they would kill many in the future because there was no mercy in their eyes.

CHAPTER SIX

CAUGHT BETWEEN THE LINES

The sun rose, but I was still awake. My mom knocked on my room door. I opened it. The moment she saw me, she knew that I hadn't slept at all. She hugged me and asked me to come to the dining room after bathing. Then she went to the kitchen. I was still thinking about my murders, but I pushed myself up and went to the bathroom. I took off my clothes and turned on the shower. I closed my eyes, but my inner thoughts didn't let me find peace. I was hallucinating that the shower was showering blood instead of water when I closed my eyes. In shock, I opened my eyes and took a deep breath. After showering, I changed my clothes and went to the dining room.

I sat at the table. I saw my mom cooking breakfast. She noticed me and said, "Two minutes, Ethan." I replied, "Okay, Mom." Then she came and placed the plates on the table. She served and sat next to me. I initially refused to eat, but she insisted.

I ate half of my plate and told my mom, "I'm going to Master's House. I have a meeting there." She started to cry and begged me to stay with her. I calmed her down and promised her that I would come home in the evening. She didn't want me to be a part of the Mechanic gang. I hugged and kissed her on the forehead and said goodbye as I left in my car.

I arrived at Master's Villa, parked my car in the backyard, and entered the building. I saw Sam and Danny eating. They also noticed me. I went to them and sat next to them. Sam asked me to eat, but I refused. I asked Sam about the meeting. He said, "Master is in an important meeting with cops and politicians. So, it might take up to 30 minutes or more." "Ok, I am going to Uncle George's restaurant. Catch me up there," I spoke. Then I left Master's Villa. I didn't take my car, but I just walked to his restaurant. As usual, he welcomed me with a smile and made me sit. I sat on the chair and started to think about my life. A few minutes later, Uncle George came and sat opposite me, asking, "Why so confused, young man?" I didn't reply. I remained silent.

We were quiet for a minute, and then Uncle George said, "What's happened to you? It's your first day at work. Go with cheer, man." "I'm not happy in this job. I'm not a murderer," I said. He smiled and replied, "See, Mr. Youngblood, not everybody joined happily to this job. Their circumstances pulled them in. It's even applicable for Martin as well. Leave it. Now you are part of the Mechanic gang. Whether you like it or not, it doesn't matter. It's your fate to be a part of it. This Mechanic gang will be your armor for your entire life. If you are out of this gang, the next second the cops will shoot you like a pig. So, try to accept the reality. Don't worry about your life. You will be safe. I am sure about this. Take me as an example. I was a member of the Mechanic gang and killed many. My youth was filled with blood. But now I'm retired with privilege. This is the armor. I'm still being protected and will be protected by Mechanics. So, work for a few decades, then retire from your job. That's it." I slowly nodded my head and said, "Thanks, uncle. I'm leaving now for the meeting with Master."

As I was about to leave the restaurant, Uncle George suddenly called me and said, "Don't carry fear with you. It'll kill you. I've seen many youths who died due to their own fear. I hope you won't be on that list." I nodded my head. I entered Master's Villa and walked to the meeting room where Sam and Danny were waiting outside. Danny said, "You came on time, brother." I smiled at him and looked at the closed door of the meeting room. Soon, the door opened and many people wearing suits left the room. Then Master's accountant, Mr. Nicholas asked us to enter the room. Mr. Nicholas was a friend and accountant for Master Martin. He was very loyal to Master and talented in accounting. He had been by Master's side since he was in the Moonshine gang. We entered the room and the doors were closed.

Master Martin had some water and asked, "Is everything fine?" At first, we didn't answer, but the moment he asked that through his eyes, I said, "Fine, Master." He replied, "That's good." Then the master continued to speak. He said, "It's a new day, new life, new people. So, forget the past, especially yesterday! You and your mom will be protected by the Mechanic gang, and that's my promise. It's safe for you to be a part of us, okay?" I nodded my head. He said, "Alright, then I have a task for you. It's not a big deal."

Danny asked, "What is the job, Dad?" Master stared at him and then corrected him, saying "Master" instead of "Dad."

Master said, "It's a collection day, boys. So, Ethan, you will drive. Sam and Danny can handle the collection." He pushed a paper towards me which contained the amount and address. "The bills at the motel were a little short last month, so make sure he pays us the interest he owes." The accountant said, "Don't lay hands on anyone unless there is no other choice. Our clients need to understand that we provide a valuable service. They need to look for you and Master Martin for protection. They need to believe that you will protect them."

We nodded our heads to show that we understood everything in the meeting. Then we stood up from our chairs. As we were about to leave, Master stopped us and said, "Better be armed, Boys. Get a weapon from the pawnbroker and say that you are on duty so that he gives you arms free of cost." I said, "Sure, Master." He wished as good luck and we left the meeting room.

CHAPTER SEVEN

SUIT UP FOR TROUBLE

Sam, Danny, and I walked out of Master's Villa. We got into the car and started the engine. Sam opened the door and got in, but Danny jumped through the open window. He was very excited to be a Mechanic, but my lips didn't smile. They tried their best to cheer me up, but I remained the same.

I stopped the car in front of the pawn shop. Danny rushed to the shop and opened the door very forcibly, making the old man jump from his chair. He scolded Danny for his immature act. Then the old man asked about the purpose of our visit. "We want guns free of cost," Sam said with pride in his voice. The old man replied, "That's not my policy. I didn't give you the guns because you are Martin's son. Wipe your ass and leave." Danny burst into laughter, which made Sam steam. They had a verbal fight for a few minutes.

After that, Sam explained to the old man, "Listen, old man. Now we are Mechanics. Do you hear? MECHANICS." But suddenly, the old man picked up a half-cut double-barrel shotgun from under his desk and pointed it at Sam's head. Everyone was angered by the old man's actions. Sam and Danny started to cry and apologize for their behavior. But the old man laughed and loosened his grip on the gun. Then he said, "You young boys, grow some balls. Here are your tools." They took the revolver, but he gave me a 1911 pistol and said, "Take care, son." I was confused as to why the old man gave me a different weapon than the one he gave to them. We left the shop after signing the register.

We got in the car and started moving to the first address to collect bills. I didn't carry the gun given by the old man. Instead, I placed it on the seat next to me. Sam asked why I wasn't carrying it, but I didn't reply. Sam and Danny giggled behind me and mocked me. Then, Sam said, "Let us see, Ethan. How long have you managed to survive in this business without carrying a gun?" and laughed.

Then we reached our first address. Sam asked me to stay in the car so that the getaway process would be fast in case of an emergency. Danny and I stayed in the car.

A few minutes later, Danny got out of the car and jogged to a nearby shop. I asked him to stop, but he did not listen to me. He brought something and entered the car. I asked him, "Why did you get out of the car?" He showed me the pack of cigarettes. I was shocked and asked, "Have you ever smoked before?" He said, "No." "Then why did you bring this?" I asked. He replied, "It's a tradition. It's a fashion. Every gangster should smoke, drink, and hang out with some young titties. Do you want one?" I said, "No, you smoke, gangster. I don't want it." Then he lit a cigarette and inhaled a puff, which made him cough badly. I grabbed the cigarette from his hands and threw it outside the car.

A few minutes later, Sam came with a suitcase and entered the car. Danny asked, "Is it a green light, buddy?" Then Sam opened the suitcase, which was filled with money, making them both ecstatic. I started the car and drove to the next address. It was a smooth collection day.

Days gone. Every businessman settled the shares properly. One day, as usual, we went for collections. Sam and Danny started to smoke in the car. I asked them to throw out the cigarettes from my car, but they were too distracted by the money and smoke. We only had two more client addresses left. Sam pointed out that we left beer warehouse, which is outside the city. Then I drove to that location.

Finally, we reached the beer warehouse. As usual, Sam went to collect the bill. Meanwhile, Danny and I were sitting in the car. Danny was practicing smoking without coughing, but he coughed every time. We waited for nearly five minutes and began to panic about Sam and his situation. Suddenly, we heard a gun sound and Sam screaming in pain. Sam was shouting, "Ethan...Danny..." We got out of the car and went near the main door where we saw Sam had been shot and was struggling to crawl. We rushed to him but he told me, "Ethan, catch the motherfucker. He is escaping. Catch him, Ethan." I nodded my head to him and rushed to my car and started it. The guy drove his car from the garage near the beer warehouse and tried to escape from us.

I chased him for a very long time. He tried to kill me by shooting, but in vain because all the bullets he shot only hit my car. Fortunately, nothing hit me. I continued to chase him. At some point, when he tried to turn sharply right, his car lost control and flipped upside down. I stepped out of my car and went near the car with the pistol for safety.

The guy somehow managed to come outside of the flipped car by crawling. His right hand was cut in half. He had a deep wound in his back. He seemed like his entire body was soaked in blood from head to toe. He looked red. I asked him, "Why did you try to escape from us? It is just a regular collection, right? Then why did you try to flee from us?" He said, "I am not the owner or a worker of the beer warehouse. I am from the Iron gang. We were trying to capture the people in your security. But now I am going to die." I said, "Don't worry. I will take you to the hospital." He replied, "I am bleeding. Half of my blood is running on the road. It's nearly impossible to save me. Even if you manage to save me, Father will kill me for failing in my job. Ahhhh, it's painful like hell. If you want to help me, put a bullet in my head." I said, "No, I can't." He begged me for death, but I didn't shoot him. Instead, I tried to lift him. I grabbed his left hand and tried to drag him out. But before he could make it out, his life had ended.

Filled with guilt, I couldn't focus on anything that day. I somehow managed to get into my car, as my mind was in a haze. I then drove to the beer warehouse and entered. The actual owner of the warehouse informed me that Sam had been taken to the hospital and mentioned that he had been shot in the leg. So, Sam's life was safe.

I then went to the hospital where the warehouse owner had mentioned Sam was admitted, but he was not there. I was confused and at a loss. Suddenly, an old man informed me that Sam was at the doctor's house, which was near Master's Villa. I asked, "Thank you, Sir but who are you?" He replied, "Ex-Mechanic. Now, carpenter. Sorry, I have to leave. See you around." I was speechless at that time.

Then I took my car and went to the Doctor's house where Sam was being treated by a doctor named Richard Cavill. After meeting him, I came to know that every Mechanic would come to him whenever they were injured, and he is considered as the only Doctor in our territory.

I asked Sam about his pain, but he pretended not to have any and said, "It is common in gangster life." The doctor finished his treatment, and I asked about the fee, but he said, "It is free for all Mechanics and their families." I thanked him for treating Sam. Then I took both brothers to their house. I decided to hide Sam's wound from my mom because I thought it would only make her worry more about me. I started the engine and reached my home as I promised my mom.

I opened the main door of my home and entered. My mom was waiting for me, sitting on the couch, and ran to me when she saw me. She held my hands and led me to the garage. Pointing out my father's workbench, she said, "Do you know this place? Right?" I nodded my head. "It's your father's place. Most of his time was spent at this workbench. So please remember that. You have a space to work and mom to take care of. I know what happened to Sam. Don't ever try to hide things from me, boy. I'm your mother. Keep that in your mind. You are bad at hiding things, Ethan. After I got married to your father, I was very concerned about his life. So, one day when he was working at his workbench, I came and sat on his lap and asked him to promise me that he would come home safely every day. He made the promise and followed it strictly. But unfortunately, he was killed. So, I want you to promise me the same and follow it." I hugged her and said, "I promise you, mom."

CHAPTER EIGHT

MELODY OF LIFE

After our first job, we were not given any major tasks by the master for many days. Danny and I used to accompany the master as bodyguards when he went to other places for meetings. Sam was not completely healed at that time, so he did not come with us when we went to do the gang's work, but he did accompany us when we went to Uncle George's restaurant. We loved Uncle George and his company.

It was a usual sunny day. I finished my delicious breakfast and took my car to the master's villa. I waited in the main hall where Danny and Sam were sitting. After waiting for 20 minutes, we went to our regular spot, Uncle George's restaurant. We had a fun time with Uncle George. It was a fun day. We sat there till 4:45 PM. Then Danny and Sam went to their house. I was about to leave the restaurant, but Uncle George called me over to the counter where he was sitting. I asked him, "What, Mr. Fatty Uncle?" (In a fun tone). He looked around to ensure nobody was near us, then he said, "Look, I have a daughter." I was shocked and shouted, "What?" He tried to calm me down and said, "Yes, I have a daughter, but she is not in this town. I have kept my family safely in another town called 'Aqua Vista'. 15 years before, my wife eloped with a Carpenter in that town, so I gave my daughter to a Church father to raise her. I used to visit my daughter only three times a year. I promised her that I would take her with me when she reached 18. But two days before, she telephoned me and said that she was coming to Moonshine Town and decided to settle here with me. She had not yet reached 18 and was very adamant like me. Now she is on her way by train. By tomorrow at 12 noon, she will arrive at the Moonshine railway station.

I was clueless as to why he was narrating these stories to me, so I asked him. He said, "I want you to safely take my daughter to me because there are many rogues in the surrounding area of the railway station. So please, bring my daughter safely to me. Please, son. Don't say no." I replied, "I am okay with this, but I might have work tomorrow with the master." He laughed and said, "Don't worry about him. I already spoke to Martin this morning. He has no problem with this. Are you okay with it or do you have other plans?" and laughed loudly. I said, "Fine, I will safely deliver your stubborn package to you." His laughter continued as he gave me the details of his daughter. I grabbed them and put them in my pocket.

I exited the restaurant and drove my car home, parking it in the garage. As I entered, I noticed a pleasant fragrance. I called my mom to ask about it, and she informed me that it was a perfume she had bought from the pawn shop. When I questioned why she had gone there, she explained that she had accompanied Aunt Terese who wanted to pawn something. She then mentioned that she had come across the perfume bottle and thought I would like it, despite my reluctance to use such products. After a brief exchange, she threw the bottle at me, insisting me to use it.

Later on, I decided to repaint my cars in red and began preparing everything in the garage. However, my mom intervened, reminding me that the cars belonged to her darling and should not be repainted. I begrudgingly rearranged everything and returned home, where I turned on the TV to watch some programs. From upstairs, my mom called my name and scolded me for not checking the pockets of the clothes before putting them in the wash. She then handed me a piece of paper that Uncle George had given her, prompting my curiosity about its contents.

I took the piece of paper to the couch. My mom rushed to me and sat next to me in the same couch. I unfolded it and saw the name "Abigail". My mom grabbed the paper from me, read it, and asked, "Who is she, Ethan? Is she your girlfriend?" I replied, "Mom, Uncle George gave it to me. Abigail is his daughter. He wanted me to pick her up at Moonshine Railway Station by 12 noon." After hearing this, my mom began to tease me and said, "I think she will be your girlfriend." I calmed my mom's imagination and helped her with dinner. While eating, my mom insisted that I use perfume the next day. Reluctantly, I agreed. After finishing dinner, I went to my room and slept.

I was in a deep sleep when my mom woke me up and said, "It's time, boy. Wake up." I managed to open my eyes and saw that it was 8:15 AM. I was frustrated by my mom's behavior and told her, "Mom, it's only 8:15. Please let me sleep." She rushed to my room and said, "You have to pick up a girl, Ethan. Hurry up." I replied, "Mom, she is coming at 12 o'clock. It's only 8:15 now." She responded, "So what? Get up, freshen up, and eat breakfast. Wait for her at the railway station. It won't hurt to wait for a girl, Ethan." I took a deep breath and said, "Fine, mom. I will wait for her." She said, "Good," and I went to the bathroom.

After I came out of the bathroom, my mom shouted my name and said, "Ethan, I have chosen an outfit for you and kept it on your bed. Wear it." I was clueless as to why she was doing this. I thought it was some sort of prank or a setup for a taxi service. Despite my reluctance, I accepted to wear the outfit which turned out to be my dad's. I entered my room and saw a long suit on the bed. Frustrated, I reluctantly put it on, unable to do anything about it. As I came down to the dining room, my mom was speechless seeing me in the suit. It was my first time wearing such formal attire. She hugged and kissed me, telling me how handsome I looked.

We sat down to eat breakfast, and after finishing, I grabbed my car keys to leave the house. However, my mom stopped me, spraying perfume on me and giving me a hat to wear. I followed her instructions and finally left the house.

As I started the engine and said goodbye to my mom, I didn't think about Abigail at all while driving to the railway station. But as I arrived and waited for her, my mind was filled with questions. What would she look like? Short or tall? Modern or tribal? Friendly or arrogant? I lost my patience and repeatedly asked the station master about the train's arrival, unable to keep still. Finally, I heard the sound of a train horn in the distance. I rushed to the platform and waited for her anxiously.

Finally, the train stopped. Everybody on the train began to depart because it was the last stop. I was confused because there were too many girls out there. So, I shouted, "ABIGAIL....ABIGAIL..." But I wasn't able to find her. Suddenly, I felt a touch on my back, so I turned around. I saw a gorgeous girl standing in front of me. I was stunned by her beauty. She was nearly my height with a side-swept twist hairstyle. She wore a short red frock with white dots.

She was so sexy with her pinkish lips and the moment I saw her; she stole my heart. She said, "I am Abigail. Are you the driver sent by my father, George?" What a voice. It was the sweetest voice I had ever heard. But I felt a pang of pain when she called me a driver, so I said, "Ms. Abigail, I am not a driver. I am a friend of your father. He is more like an uncle to me." She quietly said, "Sorry. I thought you were the driver." I replied, "It's okay, Ms. Abigail. Give me your luggage and wait next to the red car outside the station." As I said this, she went to my car.

I took her luggage and walked out of the station. I neared the car and was about to place the luggage on the ground to open the car door, but she stopped me and said, "Don't place my luggage on the ground. It'll get dirty." I looked at her and said, "Then how can I open the door, madam? The car key is in my suit's pocket." She asked, "In which pocket?" I said, "My right bottom pocket. "She didn't wait for a second. She just put her hand inside my pocket and searched for keys. She was very close to me. She smelled good. It wasn't a perfume smell; it was her own scent. I wished to enjoy her fragrance a little longer, but she quickly found the keys and opened the door. I then placed the luggage on the back seat, leaving no room for her to sit. I wanted her to sit next to me in the co-pilot seat. As I had hoped, she sat next to me. At that moment, I felt like the happiest person in the world.

I started driving to Uncle George's restaurant. On the way, she asked for my name. I replied, "Harold Ethan," to which she responded, "Nice name." I tried to hide my blushes. She then inquired about the relationship between me and her father, and I answered her question. She asked me to stop the car at a nearby clothing store, and I obliged. She browsed through shirts while I waited on the couch in the shop. She selected some clothes and handed them to me to carry. The distance to the car was not far, but she still gave the clothes to me to carry. We got back into the car, and I didn't feel any anger. I was enjoying her company and her activities.

Then, we finally reached her stop. She opened the door and rushed to hug her father, but in the meantime, I took off all her luggage inside the restaurant and placed it on the couch. After I was done with the luggage, Uncle George thanked me. I didn't expect thanks from him but from her. I waited for her thanks. As I expected, she said, "Thank you, Ethan." I felt refreshed and exited the place. Then I drove my car to my home.

I reached my home and called my mom out of happiness. She came to me and asked, "What happened, Ethan?" "I like that girl, mom.", I said. She replied, "Are you talking about George's daughter, 'Abigail'?" I nodded my head. My mom was very happy and hugged me. She said, "If you like her, say it to her. But not tomorrow, wait for some days and wait for the right time, then propose to her." I said, "Okay, mom. Love you," and I kissed her.

CHAPTER NINE

HOT CAR

I woke up from my bed and freshened up. I asked my mom to give me all the outfits of my dad. With a smile on her face, she gave them to me. I wore a navy-blue shirt and went to Master's Villa. Sam and Danny were stunned when they saw me in that attire. They came to me and appreciated my look. Danny rushed to his room to change his clothes to match mine. After Danny went, Sam also did the same. It was hilarious. After a few minutes, Sam came wearing a black long suit and Danny with a dark green long suit.

All three were in suits. Every Master's man took a look at us. We were sitting on the couch in the waiting hall. Unexpectedly, Mr. Nicholas came to us and said, "Hey, three suit men. I have a job for you." Both Sam and Danny jumped in excitement, but I was not happy with it. I thought that if I had controlled my anger, I would be working in my garage and earning money. Money mattered a lot to me. After I killed them, my mom and I managed to live with my father's savings. Mr. Nicholas said, "Mr. David has a car repair shop in West Mount St. He actually sells stolen cars to people. He owes us 17 grand, but he wasn't able to repay it. If he had told his situation to Master, he would have been offered a full discount, but he approached Joseph. So, burn his shop in broad daylight. We have to show the power of Master Martin to the people and that lucky bastard." Sam said, "Yes, finally we got a job after a long time." "Get your Molotov from the old man and you will be paid 1 grand each.", said Mr. Nicholas. I felt happy to hear about the money. A grand. It's a huge amount. So, I said, "Don't worry, Mr. Nicholas. It's on me," and left the place. Sam and Danny followed me.

We all entered the car and I drove to the old man's shop. When I reached it, I entered the shop. When the old man saw us, he stood from his chair and asked us to follow him. We did as he said. We then reached an open space that looked like a shooting range. He asked us to wait in the shooting range. Then, after a few minutes, he came with a box full of opened wine bottles. Sam picked a bottle and was about to drink the liquid inside, thinking it was actual wine. The old man stopped him and said, "It's not wine, it's kerosene, stink ass. Now, do you still want to drink it?" Sam was shocked and said, "Fuck. I could have almost died. I don't want it, you old ass."

The old man placed the box on the table near us and picked up a bottle. He took a piece of fabric from his pocket and inserted half of it inside the bottle, leaving the other half hanging outside. He then came to us and said, "Now, it is a Molotov. An easy, hot, sexy, dangerous homemade instant weapon. Come closer, boys." He moved to the line and stood straight towards the target, instructing us to light the fabric outside the bottle and then throw the bottle on any surface so that it will broke and the kerosene would catch fire. He demonstrated this and a huge fire erupted in front of us. He then asked us to pour sand over the flame to stop it before leaving the place.

We found it difficult to put out the fire but managed to do so. We then went to find the old man.

The old man was sitting in his chair with the box on his lap. He insisted that we sign the register. Sam asked for rifles, but the old man refused to give them and said, "The panel only allotted Molotov for you. Maybe in the future, you may expect rifles. Try to manage with Molotov and side arms that I gave you before." We then signed it and got into the car.

I drove to the location that Mr. Nicholas said. Sam and Danny were ranting about their insults. They were not able to digest that they were not provided with rifles. I stopped the car near the repair shop and asked them to stop the rant and to focus on the task. Then I said, "Look, we need a distraction to finish this job. Sam, you are going to distract them. The main gate is locked from the inside. So, it will take time for them to open the gate when the garage is on fire. And Danny, you are with me." Then I asked Danny to follow me while carrying the box.

As I said, Sam got the attention of the people inside the garage. Danny and I went to the back side of the building. There was a fire escape in the back side of the building with a ladder. But the swing-out ladder was a little above my height, so I wasn't able to climb up there. I asked Danny to lift me to reach the ladder. As I said, Danny helped me reach the ladder and I released the ladder down for Danny. I helped him carry the box as he climbed up. Eventually, we both reached the fire escape. From the fire escape, we heard the voice of Sam. We tried to open the fire escape door, but it was locked. So, I took my gun and broke the glass of the door, opening it from the outside. We were very lucky that the glass-breaking noise was not heard by them due to the vehicles passing by.

I looked at Sam and the men around him. I checked for people inside the garage and thankfully, no one was there. I asked Danny to insert the fabrics on all the bottles as per old man's instructions. After the Molotov cocktails were prepared, we took them in our hands and I asked Danny for his lighter. We lit each bottle and prepared them. I counted to three and asked Danny to throw the bottles on three. We quickly threw all the bottles onto every car inside and the walls of the garage before the garage men could sense the fire. We finished the entire box of Molotov cocktails. The garage men then saw us and tried to open the main gate, but the key was inside the garage, which was almost melted by the fire.

Sam managed to escape from the gunshots and hid on the right side of my car. Danny and I jumped to the ground and ran to the car. We were all shivering in fear, but I managed to start the car and drive it away from the garage. After a few minutes, our breath returned to us and we reached Master's Villa.

We got out of the car and entered the building. We saw that the meeting room door open, and Nicholas was standing next to Master. After he saw us, he asked us to come in. Master Martin, Nicholas, and two unknown people were sitting in the room. When the Master saw us, he stood from his chair and walked towards us. He hugged us and said, "Proud of you, sons! You guys did it very well! I appreciate that! From now on, you guys should stay close to me. Whenever and wherever I go, you should come along with me. Is that clear?" We said, "Clear, Master." Then, He asked Nicholas to give us the cash. He gave us three envelopes. Sam and Danny got theirs first, and I got mine at last. When Master gave me the envelope, he told me, "I can see your potential, Ethan. You are like your father, the best getaway man I have ever seen. From tomorrow, you are my getaway man." I thanked him and left the place. I opened the envelope when I walked to my car and I was shocked to find 5 grand inside it. I was very happy at that time, so I went to Uncle George's restaurant to buy dinner for my mom.

When I entered, there was no one at the counter. So, I sat in my regular seat and waited for Uncle George, but he didn't come. Instead, my Abigail came. I was surprised with a blush on my face. She saw me and smiled. She asked, "What do you want, Ethan?" I said, "Fried chicken wings." She took the order from me and went inside the kitchen. I thought that she would come only after my order was ready, but fortunately, Uncle George was the one cooking in the kitchen. So, Abigail arrived within a minute and sat at the counter. I wanted to talk to her, so I sat in the chair right in front of her.

I was little nervous to start the conversation. I was preparing my speech in my mind and I was not ready for it. However, she started the conversation. She asked, "Then, what's up, Ethan? How is your job?" I replied, "It's good." She responded, "Oh... That's great. What about your family?" I said, "It's just me and my mom. We live on Heaven Street. What about you?" She began to tell me her story, which I already knew. In the meantime, I was enjoying her beauty and her voice. Her lips were so fresh, and she looked very beautiful without cosmetics.

After finishing her story, I asked for her address. She smiled at me and gave me her address, which I also already knew. Then she gave me my order and exchanged greetings with a smile on her lips. I went home and narrated everything to my mom.

CHAPTER TEN

PEACE RENEWAL

I went to Master's Villa at 9:30 AM and waited outside the meeting room with Sam and Danny. We waited for 10 to 15 minutes, and then Master Martin came out with Mr. Nicholas. We followed them to his car, a 4-seater black V16 Cadillac, which was a huge car at that time. The car had a natural gangster look to it, which was like a dream for me as I love Cadillacs. Master's car was always guarded by two 4-seater black 770 Mercedes-Benz cars, one in front and one in back. I was stopped walking when I saw the cars, but Sam dragged me to Master's car. Master, Sam, Danny, and Nicholas boarded the car, but my eyes still could not believe what they were seeing. They were all brand-new models launched in 1930.

Master called my name and asked me to drive the car. I sat in the driver's seat, feeling like I was on a cruise ship. Master asked me to drive the car for a second time, knowing that I loved cars and especially his car. I drove the car to the gate of the villa and asked Master where we were going. He replied, "Drive to the Grand Spencer Hotel, Ethan." As instructed, I drove to the location. While we were traveling, Master lit his cigarette and smoked. He then asked me, "Do you know why we are going to the Grand

Spencer Hotel?" I replied, "No, Master." He then began to narrate the reason for Sam, Danny, and me, saying, "It is for peace renewal, my sons. You know that the peace contract we had with the Iron gang was broken. After that, we had many gang wars, many deaths, and many orphans again. So, the police department decided to renew the peace treaty to maintain law and order between us and the Iron tribes." I had a question, so I asked, "Why is the meeting going to happen in a public place rather than the police station? Is it safe out there, Master?"

Master replied, "It's clear and clean, Ethan. So, no worries." Then we had a silent time for a few minutes. After that awkward silence, Master asked me, "Ethan, do you feel inferior to be the getaway man?" I replied, "No, Master." He then said, "Your father was a good and loyal man. He used to be my getaway man. When I saw you in the driver's seat, it reminded me of your father. You are a very important member of every mission. You are the hope for our families who rely on you to bring their family members safely to them. And one more thing. Your job is not just driving. You are among us, the gunman. You will be given a Tommy and you are going to be my support defender." I replied, "Yes, Master. I don't have a problem being a driver for you." He then nodded his head.

Finally, we reached our destination, the Grand Spencer Hotel, which was closed to the public that day. It was the biggest commercial building of that time, with a 22-story building. We didn't park our vehicles in the parking lot; instead, we were asked to park right before the main entrance. More than 30 police officers were standing outside the hotel. I wondered how many police could have been inside the building. At that time, Nicholas called everyone to look at him. Then he asked us to take four pistol magazines that suit for 1911 from the wooden box he held in his hands and asked us to replace revolvers with pistols. they all, including Master, took the guns and ammunition. Then we got out of the car and went to the boot of the car. Nicholas opened it and got five Thompson guns for us. I was stunned to see these kinds of guns and little excited to hold them. Mr. Nicholas also gave us three drum magazines each.

Then we entered the hotel, which looked like a palace. I was very excited to hold such a big gun in my hand. At that time, I forgot my fear for my life. I felt like a gangster for a few minutes. We reached the 2nd floor. Then a policeman greeted us and guided us to the meeting room. His name was Lieutenant Jacob Daniel, the man behind the meeting. He was the Controller of the entire Moonshine. The meeting room was closed from the inside. There were two policemen with shotguns. When they saw Lieutenant Jacob, they knocked on the door in a rhythmic pattern, which seemed like a code to notify the insiders to acknowledge that authorized people were waiting outside to get in. Then the door was opened.

We entered the meeting room with guns. I was the last to enter the room. It was a huge room, with nearly 20 people inside. First, the lieutenant asked Master to sit. Then he asked us to hand over all our weapons to them. They checked our entire bodies as well. I asked the guard who checked us whether Joseph and his companions were checked or not. They replied, "Yes, sir. We checked them before you arrived. "I replied, "No, officer. I do not trust you. I want them to be checked now in front of us. Right now." Upon hearing this, Joseph and his sons became heated, but the Lieutenant convinced them to undergo a weapon check. They complied, and we confirmed that they were not carrying any weapons, but Master, Sam, and I had hidden pocket knives in our shoes. After the check, Master sat down and asked us to join him. The Lieutenant sat in the middle seat as the peacekeeper, with Joseph and his sons sitting opposite us. We could hear Joseph's sons murmuring. I sat next to Master Martin, and before the meeting started, he touched my lap and whispered, "Keep an eye on the surroundings and these troublemakers. Be ready with your knife in case of any trouble." I nodded and replied, "Roger that, Master."

A few minutes later, the Lieutenant began the meeting and greeted Master Martin and Joseph. He expressed his happiness at seeing them at the peace meeting and mentioned the broken peace treaty between the Iron gang and the Mechanic gang, leading to the loss of lives, including innocent civilians. He emphasized the need to stop the fights and restore mutual peace through racing sports.

Master Martin agreed to renew the peace treaty without hesitation, but Joseph refused, advocating for gang wars and violence instead. The Lieutenant said, "Gentlemen, it's not only beneficial for one side. It's for both sides. See, we already lost many. Hereafter, we don't want to lose anyone in the name of vengeance. It's the month of December. We have Halloween, Christmas, and New Year. So please, try to understand, Mr. Joseph. The police need some rest and time to spend with family in this month." Joseph then agreed to sign the treaty. After a few minutes, they signed the treaty, but Joseph left the room unhappy with his sons and men.

Master asked Mr. Nicholas to bring him his suitcase. As requested, Mr. Nicholas brought it to him. Master opened it, revealing that it was full of new currencies. He distributed the money to each policeman and said, "Let's celebrate this festive month with our families and friends. We will have a Christmas party at my house, so you should all come with your families." The police who had retrieved our guns returned them to us. We then left the hotel and got into the car. Master instructed me to drive to his house, which I did.

Upon reaching his house, he asked the three of us to come to the meeting room where another suitcase was placed on the table. He said, "Today, you guys showed me that you have patience with you. Even I struggle to control my anger. When I saw him, my eyes turned red. But you all maintained your composure. Well done, boys. From tomorrow, you will be on paid leave. You will only return to work after the new year. "After finishing his speech, he opened the suitcase and gave 4 bundles of cash to each of us, saying, "Happy holidays, boys. Be with your families. Ethan, come here often. You are one of my family. Sandra will not feel good without you. Come here. We'll go for hunting, fishing, and to the firing range." I replied, "Okay, Master. Thank you for your gift." I then left his villa, wishing them all a happy holiday.

CREATING FAMILY

It was Christmas month, and every Mechanic felt happy and enjoyed their holidays with family. It was one of the happiest phases of my life. I still remembered it as if it were yesterday, celebrating some sad Christmas without my father. Our Christmas was very dull in his absence, filled with sorrow and emptiness. My mom and I were so worried about the Christmas of 1930, not knowing that a new family was about to be created.

For the entire history of our town, we didn't celebrate as a huge party. So, Master planned to change December into a party month. Every day was scheduled with a proper plan to execute. The festivities that were not celebrated that year were also planned to be celebrated in December. Everyone in town was filled with joy and excitement.

It was a cold day on December 4th. As I was on holiday, I woke up late in the morning. But that day, I heard a deafening horn sound right by my ear. I jumped out of bed. It was 8 AM and I struggled to open my eyes. When I managed to open them, I saw the three dogs, Bruce, Sam, and Danny, laughing at me for jumping in bed. I swore at them for using a party horn to wake me up, and they stopped laughing. I asked them the reason for their visit.

Sam said, "Buddy, it's December. We have parties, Halloween, Christmas, fun, girls, and barrels of beer from ships. But you are sleeping like a pig." I didn't reply; I went to the washroom and shut the door. He was shouting from outside like a stray dog, but I didn't listen. A few minutes later, I came out of the washroom and walked to the dining room where both the brothers were sitting. I knew that Sam and Danny were upset with me. Sam again insisted that I join in the festivities, but I told him, "We still linger where my father left us, Sam. I don't know how we are going to overcome this. It's been three years since my father's death. It won't work, buddy. Leave me alone. I don't want to attend any parties." Then I walked to my garage, but they followed me. They tried to convince me, but they couldn't.

Suddenly, my mom came to us and inquired about our conversation. She was pushed into the memory of her beloved husband and shed tears when she heard what we were talking about. Sam and Danny convinced my mom and made her say, "Ethan, let this be a new start. "Then I accepted the invitation of Sam and Danny. We had breakfast at our home, as usual, it was delicious. Then they took me with them and asked my mom to come in the evening. They took me to Master's Villa. We entered the Villa, and it seemed different. The entire Villa was decorated. The villa had been transformed into a children's park, a party hall, and a stage to entertain people. I was amazed to see the arrangements that were all made by them. We walked to the backyard of the villa where we found Master Martin playing with kids like a kid. It was then that I realized Master was very fond of children. He saw us and his face was automatically filled with joy and happiness. He hugged us tightly and then asked us to accompany him with the kids. We played like children for almost one and a half hours. When we all felt tired, Master said that he was going to take a nap in his room. However, we went to Uncle George's restaurant to eat something.

Uncle George's Restaurant was filled with customers and we had no space to sit. Uncle George placed many chairs and tables outside his restaurant for the overflow of customers. When he saw us standing outside, he came out and hugged us in fulfilled happiness. He grabbed our hands and dragged us to the backside of the restaurant where he had special tables for special customers. I knew that place. It once seemed like garbage, but now it was decorated with warm lights and a roofed fan. He made us sit there and said, "First, eat what you want. Then, Uncle has work for you. Go and tell your orders to Abigail. She is in the kitchen. Sorry, I have customers to serve. First, eat. Then, Abigail will give you the task." Then he left the spot.

I was very happy to know that Abigail was there. So, I wanted to meet her privately. I was thinking of an idea when Sam volunteered and gave me a wonderful idea. He said, "Guys, one of us should go to Abigail and place the order. I won't go there. It's too smoky inside."

My heart raced to get into the kitchen so I quickly stood up from the chair which gained their attention. I somehow acted like I was in a normal state, but I wasn't. I reached the entrance of the kitchen. She was standing in the corner of the kitchen in front of the stove. She wore a short blue frock with an apron tied in the back. Her neck was glistening with sweat drops. She made me feel like I was in some unrealistic land. She was very beautiful and sexy. When I saw her, my eyes blurred everything around her, and I didn't even hear anything. Suddenly, my mini dream was shattered by a server who shouted at me to make space for him to enter the kitchen. The sound made by the server caught Abigail's attention. She turned her head and looked at me. She looked stunning. We had beautiful eye contact for a few seconds. Then she raised her eyebrows and asked about my visit.

My heartbeat raced, but I somehow managed to calm myself and went to her. She asked me, "Ethan, what are you doing here? It's too smoky. Go and sit inside. Waiters will come to you." I was completely blank, and no words came from my mouth. She touched my shoulder and asked, "Ethan, are you okay?" Then I came back to the normal world and took a long breath in. She once again repeated the same question because she knew that I hadn't been myself. I said, "No, Miss. I'm alright. I like to be here." She thought for a second and asked, "Okay... what do you want to eat? Make your order." But I forgot what they said, so I told her to prepare every dish on the menu. She was shocked and very doubtful, so she repeated what I said, "Everything on the menu, right?" I nodded my head, and then she confirmed the orders. She placed the pan on the burner and poured some oil. She was a well-skilled cook with style. I loved the way she sautéed the dish. I just enjoyed the way she cooked and looked. But as she was cooking, she simultaneously started a conversation. She asked, "Well, what's your plan for tonight?" I didn't understand what she was talking about, so I asked her to repeat what she had said. She repeated the same thing, but I was confused because I didn't know what was going to happen that night.

She realised that I wasn't aware of the events for that night, so she said, "We have a party tonight. Every Mechanic is going to attend it." I was very nervous at that moment because I am not good at these kinds of social events. I nodded without saying a word. Abigail noticed that I was not interested in parties and tried to convince me, but I kept lying to her about having work. She knew I was lying. She then said, "It's a dance party, young Mechanics should come as a pair. I thought we could attend the party together, but it's okay, I will find another guy." She turned to the stove and started cooking. I felt both excited and worried because I had told her I would never attend the party, but my heart urged me to go with her. So, without hesitation, I said, "I will come." She asked, "What?" I repeated, "I will come with you as a pair." She smiled at me, her eyes expressing excitement. She blushed and said, "Then it's fine. I'm going to wear a white cross-back gown. What about you?" Without hesitate, I said, "I will wear a red dress." She asked, "Red? What shade of red?" I replied, "I have no idea because I am very bad at dressing, even now my mom chooses my outfit."

She said, "Oh my God! You are a grown kid, Ethan. Okay, that's fine. Then go and tell Aunt Margaret about this party. She will help you out, but try to come in black or white." I replied, "Okay, miss." She did not like the way I addressed her, so she asked me to call her Abigail. Then she said, "You have to pick me up from my home for the party. Come by 6:30 in the evening." I nodded my head with a controlled smile filled with excitement and love. She gave me more instructions, saying, "Don't pick me up in the red car. I know you have a cream-colored car in your garage. Get that for me. Okay?" Without hesitation, I agreed. I asked, "How do you know I have a cream-colored car? You've never been to my house, so how do you know?" She giggled and said, "Your mom and I go to the same church. She's told me a lot about Uncle Ben and you, but I've never seen you there. I think you don't have time to visit, but you did have time to bomb the back wall once." She laughed. I was very surprised that she knew about my childhood, even though I didn't know her favorite color was white. I was shocked that even my mom hadn't mentioned their friendship.

Then I was about to ask her something, but she stopped me and said, "Keep it for tonight, Ethan. We have enough time to talk at the party, but now I have work to do. Your order will arrive at your table. Go and eat it. See you this evening." Then she started cooking the orders and I left the kitchen after exchanging greetings.

I went to Sam and Danny, who were clueless about why I had been gone for so long. Danny asked about the delay, but I managed to divert their attention from the topic. I lied to them, saying that Abigail had given me an important task to do, and they believed me. Soon, our orders arrived at our table. Sam and Danny were shocked to see 17 plates of dishes on our table. I told them, "Guys, it's a special day. We can eat as much as we want and take the leftovers home." Then we started eating. The food was amazing and delicious, making us eat until we were full, leaving no trace of food on the plates. After finishing our lunch, we went home.

I parked my car and entered my house. My mom was sitting on the couch, doing some handicraft work. I sat next to her and asked, "Does Abigail come to church regularly?" Without even looking at me, she replied, "Yes."

I asked, "Have you become friends?" Then she looked at me and said, "Yes, Ethan." I was shocked and asked her, "Did you share our family and my childhood things with her?" She nodded her head. I felt slightly upset because my mom shared everything with me. So, I asked, "Then why didn't you share these things with me, mom?" She set aside her handicraft things on the table and held my hands. She said, "I am sorry, darling. But Abigail didn't want me to share our relationship details with you. I think she is also interested in you and she only inquired about your past and your character." I was jumping around because I was very happy to know that she also had an interest in me, but my mom stopped me and said, "Wait, Ethan. I am not sure about her intentions. So, wait for some time, okay? Why are you asking all these questions? Who told her about our church visit?" I told my mom, "Abigail. She told me and she wants me to be her date at tonight's party. She said that all the young Mechanics should come in pairs. So, we are going together. She asked me to wear something in black or white." My mom was so happy to hear that and hugged me tightly. Then I said, "Do you know one thing? She wants me to pick her up from her home. She asked me to come in the cream-colored car in our garage." My mom was confused by her description, but I told her, "Mom, it's a Mercedes 400." Then she understood what Abigail meant. My mom then asked me to clean the car while she searched for an outfit.

I went to the garage and removed the sheet that was covering the car. It was in good condition because I used to drive it at least once a week. Then I took a piece of fabric and started to clean it. I replaced the old engine oil with new oil. Then I took the cream car and went to the gasoline station to fuel it up. I filled the entire fuel tank because of my overactive imagination that she would accept my invitation to come with me to Eve's Mountain after the party that night.

After that, I went home. I entered the house and climbed the stairs to my room where my mom was waiting for me. When she saw me, she got up from the bed and showed me a white linen suit with a brown tie. It looked good, but I didn't think it would suit me. She asked me to take a bath and wear the suit she had chosen for me. I followed her instructions.

As I descended the stairs wearing my father's outfit, my mom started to shed tears. I comforted her and she explained that I looked like my father in the suit. I reassured her and she made some adjustments to my attire. She sprayed the perfume she had bought from the old man's shop.

I was little nervous. I didn't know how to behave at a party. So I asked my mom, "Will everything go well, mom? I am nervous and my hands are ice cold." She replied, "Everything will be alright when you step into the party. Be normal. Don't act weird. And the important thing is, don't show your fear in your eyes, young man. It will ruin your romantic night with her." However, my nervousness did not seem to be under control. So, I asked, "But I can't help it, mom. It's not in my hands." She replied, "Look, honey. It's very simple. Take your car. Go to a flower shop. Buy some white flowers. It's better to fill the entire passenger seat with white flowers. Have a single white flower in your coat suit pocket. Handle it with care. It shows how you will care for her. Okay?" [Ethan nodded his head] "Good. Then go to her house. Don't honk the horn in front of her house. Park your car in front of her house even if there is a parking space. Then knock on the door three times. Not more than that. When she opens the door, compliment her beauty. When she comes to your car, open the door for her. Drive at a moderate speed or at a speed that doesn't disturb her hair. Talk with her while driving or describe her beauty. When you reach the party, open the door to let her out. Walk at the same speed that she walks. Don't rush. Then dance with her but don't step on her dress or her foot. At dinner, take her plate to fill it for her. Finally, when you drop her off at her home, wait for a moment. If you have a gut feeling that she may also have romantic feelings, slowly get closer to her and kiss her lips. [Ethan was shocked to hear this] What? This is the right time. If you sense that she is not in a romantic mood, don't try to kiss her. Okay?" With a lot of things in mind to clarify, I said, "Okay, mom."

Then I asked her, "When will you be there, mom? Because if I have any doubts, I can clarify them with you." She replied, "I will be there by 6 PM or 6:15 PM." I took a deep breath as a sigh of relief, but my questions were not finished. I asked her, "But what should I do if all of my preparations go wrong?" She smiled at me and said, "Then go with what is happening there." I was convinced by my mom's plan. I hugged and kissed her, then got into my cream car to pick up my girl. It was 5:15 PM when I got into my car and went to the flower shop. The flower shop was closed, but its back door was open and the owner was loading stock for the next day. I asked him to give me the flowers to fill the car, but he didn't want to sell flowers after the shop was closed. I tried to convince him and begged for the flowers, but nothing happened. Then I told him that I was going to a party and needed the flowers to impress my girl. When he heard this, he was ready to give me the flowers and said, "For Mechanics, anytime is business time. "I asked him to fill the entire car passenger seat with white flowers, but he said that he didn't have that many white flowers. So, I told him to fill half of the passenger seat with mixed colored flowers and the upper half with white flowers.

However, he mentioned that the pollen grains would stick to both my outfits and the edges of the car, which would smell bad in the future. Therefore, he gave me a plastic cover to cover the entire back seat, and then we filled the flowers inside. While filling the flowers, I took off my coat to avoid getting pollen grains on it. I then took a white flower and placed it in my suit pocket. After paying him a significant amount, I went to her home. It was 5:53 PM according to my watch. I parked the car as my mom had instructed me, following her directions carefully. I reached the door of her house and knocked on it three times, but there was no response. I knocked again, but she still didn't answer. I knocked third time, more forcefully, and finally, she opened the door. When I saw her, I was stunned by her beauty. She wasn't fully ready, her hair was dishevelled, flying everywhere. Her eyes, nose, lips, ears, and entire face were stunning, but her hair was messy. Despite wanting to laugh, I controlled myself and complimented her, saying, "You look good, like an angel in a white gown." She responded, "I know you're laughing inside. I'll be ready in 15 minutes. Come in and make yourself at home." It was an awkward situation because I had messed up with my words during our first encounter. I didn't compliment her properly. She knew that it was an artificial compliment that just came out of my mouth. She went inside her room and closed the door.

In the meantime, I roamed everywhere in her house except for her room. I saw every picture of her and her family that was hanging on the walls. I felt hungry, so I went to the kitchen and ate some cookies. I knew that they were prepared by Uncle George. While I was eating, she opened the door and saw me eating cookies in the kitchen like a rat. She giggled at me and said, "It's enough, Ethan. It's already late. Come." Then I returned the cookie box to where I took it from. I went near her and gave her the white flower from my pocket. She was very surprised by the single white rose and said, "How did you know that I like white roses?" I was also surprised to find out that the flower I kept in my pocket was a rose, but I maintained that I kept it intentionally. At that moment, I gained confidence, so I gently closed her eyes with my hand without disturbing her makeup. She was surprised when I closed her eyes and asked, "Ethan, what's your plan? What are you doing?" I told her, "Wait, Miss Gorgeous, there is something special waiting for you outside." She was very excited and said, "Quick, Mr. Handsome, I can't wait anymore." I then took her outside and locked the door behind us. We went near the car, and with my left hand, I opened the roof of my car. She almost guessed my surprise because of the fragrance. Then I opened her eyes.

Abigail was astonished to see a car filled with white flowers. She was very excited, but also very conscious of keeping her distance from it due to the pollen grains that could spoil her dress. She was jumping with joy, both to the sky and the ground. I was delighted to see her so impressed. In her excitement, she hugged me tightly, and I hugged her back. She stood in front of the car, gazing at the flowers for more than 10 minutes. It became clear that she wouldn't take her eyes off them without my intervention, so I gently woke her from her reverie and somehow managed to convince her to get into the car.

Once she was inside, I was thrilled as I had wanted her to join me in my car. To my surprise, she initiated the conversation and suggested that we be a pair. I then drove my car to Master's Villa, where the party was being held. The Villa was heavily guarded by Mechanics, resulting in a long line of cars waiting to enter. We were at the end of the queue. The Mechanics were thoroughly checking each car and its passengers, causing a delay. After 10 minutes, we finally reached the gates where many Mechanics were conducting the checks. They searched every nook and corner of my car, even insisting on checking the passenger seat.

I explained to them that it was filled with flowers, but they didn't believe me and proceeded to search the passenger seat as well. Despite Abigail's pleas to let us in, they ignored us. But Danny came to the spot suddenly and asked the guards to let us in. I didn't know why he came outside, but it was our luck.

Master's Villa's backyard was decorated like a party in Italy, setting a warm and romantic mood. We were the last to arrive at the party. Abigail's face looked pretty in the warm light. She also loved the party setup and said, "Ethan, it's so romantic, right?" I didn't reply to her; instead, I held her hand. It was very romantic for a third person, but for me, it was a huge risk because it could go either way - she could either slap me and leave the car or accept my touch. Fortunately, she chose the second option. At that moment, I confirmed that Abigail also had feelings for me. Her eyes spoke more than her pink lips. I parked my car in the allotted space and quickly got out, attempting to open the door for her. However, she beat me to it and opened the door herself. Even though I knew she was in love with me, I stuck to my mom's plan. I tried everything to execute my mom's plan accurately, but she didn't allow me and I didn't want to be dragged into it. So, I abandoned my plan and followed her lead.

Abigail waved her hand for me to come quickly, so I ran to her. She held my hand and said, "Come, Ethan, we can sit there." [Pointing to seats in the middle row] The moment she held my hand, I felt something different within me. When we walked to our seats holding hands, everybody's eyes were on us. I felt embraced at that party. I saw my mom sitting in the first row next to Aunt Sandra. She also looked beautiful in a red gown. I gestured to her that she looked beautiful and gave her a flying kiss. She also gave kisses back to both me and Abigail, who she didn't notice, gestured that we made a nice pair. This made my shyness and embarrassed feelings vanish.

Abigail then asked me to sit on the chair and noticed my mom watching us. When Abigail saw my mom, she gestured again to say that Abigail looked beautiful, and Abigail also gestured that my mom looked pretty.

A few minutes later, Mr. Nicholas got on the stage and said, "A great welcome to all the ladies and gentlemen seated here. Thank you for your patience. We have ball dancing, food, wine, whiskey, and barrels and barrels of beer (he laughed). But before that, Master Martin wants to say a few words to you. Have a joyful night, folks!" Then he stepped down from the stage.

Everybody at the party gave a huge applause as Master Martin stepped on the stage. When he climbed the stage, his wife, Sandra, gave him a flying kiss and loudly said, "I love you, Martin." Master Martin smiled at her and returned the flying kiss. Then he faced the people sitting before him and said, "It's a great evening for all of us. Everyone, it was once my dream, but not anymore. Because, it finally happened today. It's for all the Mechanics. It would not have been possible without you and your sacrifice." Our son, brother, father, husband, and our family sacrificed their lives to enhance our living. The women in our families are way stronger than men because they are the actual support for us. They are the masterminds for us. My wife is very sweet, lovable, and forever beautiful. Sandra is behind me, and she is the one who holds my life in her hands.

(Aunt Sandra starts weeping and her sons console her from the back) If she loses her grip on me, I will die. She controls my unnecessary anger and has made me a responsible father. (He takes a few seconds to pause) One thing I have to mention here is Mr. Benjamin James, my brother. He planted the idea of the Union party in my brain, but now I am standing alone on stage without him. His eyes are always around us, especially his family (me and my mom in the distance start to cry. Abigail consoles me, and Aunt Sandra consoles my mom). My sister Margaret and my son, Ethan, are just like his father Benjamin. He is a talented and skilled member of my close crew. [Master notices many people crying for their deceased family members] Okay, I am getting emotional and I don't want to spoil the party mood by making everyone sad. [He inhales and exhales and then says loudly] So, the party is on tonight. It's your fucking day, Mechanics. Come on!" He jumped down from the stage to Aunt Sandra and kisses her before asking his men to play some music.

Within a few seconds, Master's men put away the chairs and made room for the dancers. Abigail gave her hands and said in a romantic tone, "Let's dance, Ethan." I took her hands and we went to the center of the dance floor. I didn't know how to dance, but Abigail guided me with her movements. She made me appear as if I was an experienced dancer, but in reality, she was the puppeteer and I was tied to her invisible strings, dancing to her control. The audience began to applaud, and many of them joined us on the dance floor as couples. Even Master Martin danced with Aunt Sandra. I danced with both my mom and Aunt Sandra, who commented that Abigail and I looked like the perfect pair.

Abigail also danced with her dad and Master. After the dance, Uncle George approached me and said, "I know that you love my daughter. I will not be an obstacle to your love. I like you, man, and I would be happy to have you as my daughter's husband, Ethan." I replied, "Uncle, I haven't even proposed to her yet." He responded, "So what? She loves you too. Choose the right time and propose to her." I didn't reply to him, instead, I hugged and thanked him.

Master also commented that we looked like a divine couple and hugged me. A few minutes later, Abigail returned with two plates full of dishes from the buffet. I was shocked and impressed by the way she lived her life. There were no other women in line at the buffet, but Abigail stood out as unique among common girls. Then she said, "Ethan, you lazy cow. Hold it. There is another plate for Aunt Margaret. Wait here. I'll be back in 2 minutes." After she left, my mom came to me and said, "I love her so much more than you. She is unique," and kissed my cheeks. I handed her a plate and said, "I love you, mom" [teasing her]. She lightly hit me and asked me to sit on the nearby chair.

As Abigail had said, she returned after 2 minutes and sat next to me. We enjoyed the moment, and once again I felt that my family was recreated and reshaped by Abigail. We didn't stop talking while eating our dinner. Finally, we finished our meal, which was delicious.

When I was getting ready to ask her to go out for the night, she came to me and said, "Ethan, I have to go. Tomorrow, I have to be at the restaurant. Are you coming with me?" I was speechless, but my mom managed to say to her, "I'll send him after you, Darling." She hugged my mom and walked to my car. After Abigail got into my car, I told my mom about my plan to take her out for the night, but my mom said, "It's fine, Ethan. You know she also loves you. So, wait for a while [she hugged me]. She is waiting. Take her home safely. The party isn't over, Ethan. I'll be here, so come and pick me up," and then I walked to Abigail.

I took the car and drove it to her home at a medium-fast speed. For the first few minutes, we didn't say a single word, but then she started the conversation. She asked why I was driving slowly, so I said, "It's not safe, Abe." She liked the way I addressed her, and I noticed she blushed when I called her 'Abe.' The sky was also very romantic that night. There were stars everywhere, and we could sense rain nearby. After 10 minutes, I reached her home. As usual, she came out of the car before I opened the door and stopped me from opening my side door. I asked for the reason, and she said, "Now, I have no party to attend. Can you help me get into the flower pool back there?" I smiled at her and said, "Okay." Then she let me out, and I followed behind her. I helped her by holding her hip and lifted her onto the back seat. She turned into a kid and started playing with it. After some time, I stopped her and asked her to get down. At first, she refused, but she eventually climbed out of the car on my back. We stood facing each other in awkward silence. When I tried to speak, she hugged me. However, she quickly let go and said, "Don't hesitate to come to our restaurant and kitchen." She smiled and added, "We can meet in the restaurant anytime, but come daily, okay?" I replied, "Sure, Abe." Then she waved her hand and said, "Bye, Ethan." Then she entered her home. As she was closing the door, I saw her face and eyes looking at me. I waved my hand and said goodbye without making a sound. She also nodded her head slowly before the door closed.

I got into my car and drove to my mom's house. While driving, my thoughts were consumed by Abigail. I don't even remember if I followed traffic rules during that time. When I arrived at my mom's house, I took her back to our home. During the car ride, I recounted everything that had happened that day.

CHAPTER TWELVE

SNEAK IN

The party phase was over and we were back to work. As usual, at 9:30 AM, I went to Master's villa and waited in the hall with Sam and Danny. They didn't seem to have come out of the party mood and were more interested in a party lifestyle than working. Nicholas called us in a few minutes later. Sam and Danny showed no interest in working, but I knew that their lack of interest would disappear once they were engaged in their roles as gangsters. They slowly stood up and followed me into the meeting room.

Master saw us and asked us to sit on the chairs. There was an unfamiliar figure in the meeting room who was seated next to Master. I hadn't seen him before in town or at Master's Villa. Master noticed my skepticism towards the new guy, so he introduced him to us. He said, "Well, boys, the party mood is over. We are back to business. Meet Mr. Anderson. His father worked in the Moonshine gang, but Mr. Anderson is a cop. Detective Anderson." (We were shocked to have a cop in our meeting room.) I had seen him at the meeting at the Grand Spencer Hotel. He had earned my trust and was our inside man in the police department. Another thing is that he ensured our party ran smoothly and without any issues because he kept it away from the prying eyes of his department and the public.

However, I didn't trust the cop as he seemed suspicious to me. My intuition told me that he would be trouble for us. So, I told Master, "I don't think he will be a trustworthy man to be a spy in our group. He might be a spy or even currently spying on us for Joseph. How can we consider him a fellow Mechanic?" Sam and Danny agreed with me and suggested the same to Master. But Master did not accept our opinion and said, "Trust me, boys. It's common to be suspicious of new people. But he is clean, and he has brought us valuable information." Master then looked at Anderson and asked him to explain his information. Anderson was not pleased to receive negative opinions about him on his first day in the meeting. He is not interested in explaining his intel to us at all. He said, "It's very important intel, Master. It should be handled by experts, not by amateurs." The three of us were at the peak of our temper when that insulting person underestimated us, and Sam impulsively took out his gun and fired a shot on the table out of anger. Master and Nicholas quickly intervened and calmed us down. They then warned Anderson, saying, "Anderson, you need to trust my boys because I trust them." Master then instructed Anderson to explain his intel.

Anderson began to explain, "You know that Joseph has four warehouses in his territory. Each warehouse deals with different goods. In the Darwin St warehouse, he stores illegal weapons. In the Chinatown St warehouse, he stores stolen and smuggled cars, but his car smuggling business is not very profitable. Mostly, he uses this warehouse to import and export cunts to his brothels. In Lady Roth St, he stores drugs. However, we do not know what he stores in his fourth warehouse, which is on 7th Cross St. According to the intel, he may have gold and diamonds in there. It is 99% likely to be true, but the most important thing is not the gold and diamonds. I have a serious suspicion about this particular warehouse being the war room for Joseph because I have seen him entering this warehouse several times a week, especially between 1 and 2 AM. We may face a surprise attack within a week. So, if we know what he is planning, we can prepare ourselves for a fight or take action before him."

We were consumed by a killing rage towards Joseph because he didn't stop the stupid vengeance for Mechanics. Sam and Danny were fired up to kill Joseph. Sam said, "This bastard will not stop until he's dead. We should kill him or else this will continue forever." Master did not agree with Sam's point of view because he did not see death as a definitive end to the rivalry between us. Master stopped Sam and calmed him down. He then said, "Killing Joseph will not be the end, it will only continue. Joseph will not stop the rivalry until he dies. Even after his death, his sons will continue the rivalry as a tradition. It will not stop until we erase every trace of Joseph and his gang. We need to unite and prepare a thorough plan. It is not a one-day job. We need to dismantle every brick of his fort."

We were unsure how to take down Joseph and his empire, so I asked about the plan. Anderson replied, "You should sneak into his fourth warehouse. There are Joseph's men in that warehouse. It is heavily guarded. Every night at 11:30 PM, 6 trucks enter the warehouse through the main gate after thorough checks. There are two other gates, but they are only open for Joseph. You will have to enter through the main gate. You don't have any other options." Sam asked, "How can we enter through a gate with so many guards? It's impossible." Then Anderson stopped Sam and said, "It's a tough task but not impossible. Each truck department is from a different place. Each truck has a driver and a gunman. We need to subdue them and replace them with you. Then one of you has to get into the box."

Danny laughed at Anderson's plan and said, "It's impossible. They know us. They have seen us in the meeting, Mr. Stinky ass." Anderson replied, "You kids are not that famous among Joseph's gangs. Even I don't remember you from the meeting. So do as per plan."

Danny felt insulted by Anderson, so he exited the room and Nicholas went behind him to get him back. Anderson continued, "It's our only choice. It's easy to get into the truck which departs from the Barbershop on Adam St. They have already loaded the container boxes in the barbershop. First, what you need to do is replace the stuffs in a box with one of you. Then the other two of you should wait until the two Joseph men come and reload the containers onto the truck. Then you should subdue them and take their uniforms to reduce the risk of being caught. At exactly 11:10 PM, you should drive the truck to the warehouse. When you reach the main gate, they won't check you the most, but the truck. If you successfully cross the main gate, half of our job is done. Then you need to park the truck at the side door of the warehouse. In that area, one or two men will be waiting for you. When you unload the boxes from the truck, they will count them. Inside the warehouse, it is full of bright lights. So, there is no room for you to sneak in, but each section has a monitor room near the ceiling which is connected by two-way stairs. One leads to the storage area where lights and men are present, and another stair leads to the back door. Therefore, it is best to take down the two men first. Then free up your third man who is inside the box. He should find the junction power box near the second storage section and cut the electricity supply. Enter each section of the warehouse and search inch by inch for something related to our intel. Do not take any papers or documents with you when you are leaving. Read them out there. Remember the information and report it back to Master. The most important thing is that you should carry the two men that you have knocked down in the warehouse with you because when Joseph finds out that his men were knocked down in his own warehouse, his suspicion will turn to us. So, carry them with you, including the two in the barbershop."

Sam and I were satisfied with his plan. Sam asked, "Who is going to be inside the box?" Anderson replied, "That's your problem. My job is done." We then decided to put Danny inside the box because we did not want to be inside the box for nearly 30 minutes. Anderson left the room. Master took three boxes and placed them on the table. He asked us to take one each and asked us to open it. It contained a 1911 pistol with a suppressor. The Master said, "It will not silence your fire but reduce the noise, so use it when it's needed. Be careful. I want you to meet me tomorrow. I will be waiting for you with champagne." He pushed another box to us and said, "Give this to Daniel. Explain the plan to him and convince him. Get the extra magazine from the old man."

In Master's words, I noticed a fear of losing us. I knew that he was not happy at all. Then he hugged us and sent us off. We left the room and reached Danny, convincing him by explaining the plan and giving him the new pistol with a suppressor. He agreed to come with us.

By 6:30 PM, we took a car from Master's garage and went to the barbershop on Adam's St. We parked our car in the parking lot of a cafe opposite the barbershop. We entered the cafe and sat at a window seat to spy on the barbershop. It was busy but at exactly 9 o'clock, the shop owner closed his shop and went home. I asked Sam and Danny to reach the back door of the barbershop undetected. They stood up from their seats and went there. I paid for our meal at the cafe and then went to the parking lot to get my car. I drove the car to the barbershop and parked it two shops away. Then I walked to the back door of the barbershop where Sam and Danny were clearing all the things in the box to fit Danny. The box contained mysterious items that were all wrapped in brown paper. Sam and Danny emptied the box and gave me the wrapped package to keep it safe, so I placed it in the trunk of our car. I then returned to them. Sam asked me to help him fit Danny into the box, but he was unable to fit due to his size. Sam yelled at Danny, calling him a fat ass, as he was frustrated that he should have been able to fit in the box.

However, Sam also could not fit in the box due to his height. So, the only option left was for me to get into the box. Initially, I refused to enter, but later I accepted that I was the only one who could do it. I fit perfectly in the box. Sam made a small hole in the box for ventilation and then closed the top with a wooden plate. There was no light inside, not even from the tiny hole. From outside, Sam asked, "Ethan, can you hear me?" I replied, "Yes, asshole." He then said, "Good. Listen carefully. I am going to climb onto the roof of this building. Danny will hide in the same room as you. When the two guards open the door, I will jump on one guard and Danny will take care of the other. Is that clear, Ethan?" I responded, "Yes, Sam."

Then I heard the sound of the door closing. Danny was communicating with me and conveying everything that was happening. A few seconds later, he said that Sam was climbing onto the roof of the barbershop. It was scorching inside the box and both my hands and legs were aching because I squeezed them towards my body.

After 1 hour, Danny said, "Ethan, a truck is coming to this building, man. Keep your guard up." I heard the engine sound of the truck and a few seconds later it stopped, followed by the sound of footsteps getting closer to us. Then I heard two men talking, but I couldn't make out what they were saying properly because I was inside the box like a corpse. I heard the sound of the door opening when it was opened. Then I heard a thud and a punching sound. After that, I heard some more noises after they opened the door. After a few minutes, the door was opened again. Danny said, "Finally, we did it, fuckers." Sam then opened the top of the box, allowing me to breathe properly. He asked me to stay inside the box until we reached the warehouse because it was very difficult to get into the box and it was time-consuming. So, I agreed to stay in the same place. First, they changed their outfits to uniforms, then lifted me along with the box and loaded me into the truck.

As the top of the box was not placed, I was able to see everything that Sam and Danny were doing. The boxes were quite heavy to lift with just the two of them, but I was not in a position to help them out. They finally loaded every box onto the truck. Then Sam came to me and closed the top of the box. However, Danny did not stop talking even from the passenger seat. Sam started the truck and drove to the warehouse. I did not know what was going on in the front. After a few minutes, I felt the truck turning sharply left and stopping, so I assumed that we reached the warehouse.

After a few seconds, I heard an Iron scratching sound, which was nothing but the guard opening the boot door of the truck. I was scared of getting caught, but fortunately, he didn't check properly; instead, he kicked every box with his legs. Then I heard the engine sound and felt like we were moving forward. The truck eventually stopped. When Sam and Danny were about to get down from the truck, Sam said in a low voice, "Ethan, we are going to climb down from the back of the truck." I then heard them jump out of the truck.

After a few minutes, Sam opened the top of the box and asked me to get out. When I got out, I felt like an unleashed animal from a cage experiencing freedom. I stretched my arms and legs. Sam came to me and said, "Ethan, it's time. We are at the side door of the first section. I saw no guards surrounding the first-section warehouse. So, get to the room in the warehouse first and search for the information. Then go to the junction power box near the second section warehouse. Then search the rest." I asked, "What about the storage area of the first section?" Sam replied, "We will take care of that. We are already late. So, go swiftly and come back in one piece." Then I left them.

I climbed the stairs that started from the outside of the warehouse and reached the room. It was locked but I knew how to lockpick the door. Within two minutes, I opened the door and sneaked in, searching everywhere but found nothing. I climbed down and reached the junction power box unnoticed. I cut all the wires and cables. Finally, the entire warehouse was dark. Then I searched the second section warehouse but found nothing except gold. I moved to the third section warehouse, which did not have any documents, only drug packets. Then I moved to the final warehouse. First, I searched the storage area but found nothing. So, I moved to the room on the top. Once again,

I lockpicked and opened the door, where I found a board with photos pinned to it. There were photos of Uncle George's restaurant, the church, and the flower shop. These are the famous and most crowded places near Master's Villa. Then I came to know that Joseph was planning to plant a bomb in this crowded place and wanted to kill more Mechanics. I saw a box container in the corner of the room and opened it. It contained more than 10 packs of dynamite. Using a lighter as a light source, I memorized everything on the board and then left.

I lay in the trunk of the car and successfully exited the warehouse unnoticed with the four unconscious guards, two from warehouse and another two from barbershop and drove to Master's Villa. Upon arrival, Master's men carried the four guards away and I said goodnight to Sam and Danny before leaving the Villa at 12:45 a.m. I reached home and found my mom still awake. She was a little upset with me, but I explained what had happened that day, which calmed her down. She was shocked to hear that we were in danger, but I managed to boost her courage and convinced her to go to bed.

CHAPTER THIRTEEN

THE FIRST PUNCH FOR LOVE

The next morning, I woke up and got ready. I went down to the dining area where my mom sat worried. I asked her about her concerns, and she expressed her worry about my life and the lives of the people in town due to Joseph's plan to bomb the place. I consoled her and distracted her from her worries. After having breakfast together, I headed to Master's Villa.

I entered the Villa and waited outside the meeting room with Sam and Danny. Sam and Danny asked me about what I saw that night. When I was about to tell that, Mr. Nicholas called us in. We entered and sat on the chairs. In that room, Master, Nicholas and Anderson was present. The Master gave us water and asked us to drink it. Then he said, "I'm so happy and glad to have you guys back in the house. Thank you, Christ, for bringing my sons back. Okay, Ethan, tell us what you have seen in that warehouse." I started to explain what I saw in the warehouse. I said,

"Master, we are in danger. Not only us, but the entire town, Mechanics, and their families. (Everybody in the room was shocked and worried after hearing this.) Joseph is planning to plant a bomb in Uncle George's Restaurant, the church, and the flower shop in our town. But I don't know when he is going to plant it. I saw a wooden box filled with packs of dynamite. It must contain at least ten packs of dynamite. As Anderson said it's a war room and warehouse to store gold and diamonds. We need to act quickly before that bastard, Master, or else we will witness our fellow Mechanics burning and bursting in the bomb blast." After I finished, Sam and Danny were outraged. Sam said to Master, "We can't bear this anymore, Master. We are going after every man in that gang. As you said, we are going to wipe out every member of that gang." But Master asked them to calm themselves and instructed them to sit on the chair. As he spoke, they obeyed. Then Master began to talk. He said, "Look, I know this is a tough situation. But I'm not talking about the bomb, I'm talking about the future fights that await us." Everyone was clueless about what he was talking about. So, I asked, "What are you talking about, Master?" He replied, "We can manage the bomb blast before it happens. I have a plan for that, but the problem is, it won't stop there. It will continue until one of us falls." Anderson asked, "A plan? What are you going to do, Master? Are you going to wipe out every member of the Iron gang?" Master said, "Yes, but before that, we need to finish certain things. Specifically, we need to destroy his power. First, we need to cut off the police support he has. To do that, we need to eliminate all the policemen who are under Joseph's control. Once he loses that support, we need to destroy his four warehouses on the same day. Then, we need to eliminate his sons and finally, take down that bastard."

I saw it as a great plan to bring down Joseph's entire empire. Everyone in the room agreed with the plan, but I was concerned about the bomb planting in our town. So, I asked him, "But Master, what about the bomb planted in our town and how are we going to kill the policemen? We don't have a list of them, and even if we did, how could we possibly eliminate that many policemen without raising suspicion?" For that, he said, "Don't worry about the bomb planting thing in our town. It won't happen. I'll take care of it. As for the policemen, Joseph hosts a night party at his Beach House every month. For this month, he will probably host it in the third week. But I don't know the exact date. Anderson will find out for us. Once we know the date, we can plan for it. Okay, my dear son? Go and eat something at your future father-in-law's restaurant (he smiled), you look tired." I replied with a smile, "Okay, Master. I am leaving."

Following Master's instructions, I went to Uncle George's restaurant alone because Sam had work outside of town and Danny was too tired to accompany me. When I entered the restaurant, Uncle George was in the cashier's seat. When he saw me, he stood up and came over to me. He gestured for me to sit down. His eyes were filled with worry and he was not in a normal state. I asked him about his worries and problems. At first, he hesitated to tell me but then he said, "Ethan, you know Abigail was leaving the restaurant every night after we went home. She cleans and arranges all the vessels and walks alone in the street to our home. Some bastards are making trouble for Abigail and teasing her. But yesterday, one of those bastards pulled her hand and asked her to kiss him. Abigail kicked his balls and escaped from them. I know they will wait for her again today. Can you go along with her tonight to our home? If I were 10 years younger than my current age, I would cut off all their balls and put them in their assholes and mouths. But now, I am weak. Can you help me with this, my son?"

I was very angry when I heard that and agreed to take care of these bastards. A few minutes later, Abigail came out of the kitchen and was surprised to see me. Uncle George didn't want her to know that he had asked me to accompany her, so I didn't tell her.

Abigail cooked food for me and my mom. She asked me to give it to my mom, so I said, "Okay, I'll come by evening with feedback for my mom." Then I took the food parcel and went home. I told my mom everything that had happened that day and informed her that I would be coming home late that night. She understood the situation and asked me to wait at the dining table. After a few minutes, she came with an old box. She sat next to me and opened the box. It was filled with self-defense tools from my father. She asked me to pick any tool from the box, so I chose a brass knuckleduster. Then, she gave me another tool that looked like a locket but was a mini sharp knife. She asked me to give that to Abigail for her self-defense. We then had lunch, which was simply superb. By 7:30 PM, I went to Uncle George's restaurant and waited there until Abigail closed the restaurant.

It was a full moon day. Abigail and I began to walk on the street to her home. We talked about the party night and the food that Abigail had prepared for me and my mother. She was very happy to receive good feedback from my mom. Abigail's beauty made me forget about the anger towards the bastards. That night, she wore a white shirt with a navy-blue skirt. Every white dress suited her very well. Everything went perfectly, but eventually, we saw the bastards near her home. There were four of them with beer bottles.

When they saw us, one of the bastards said, "Oh! Hey there, darling. You stepping out on us?" Abigail boldly replied, "Piss off, you shit." He then said, "Ah, hahaha, don't get your knickers in a twist, doll-face. We'll let your boyfriend watch, what do you say?" I wasn't too angry at them because they looked like kids. So, I asked, "Are we going to have trouble here?" The kid replied, "Trouble started back when you tried to steal our girl, Gentle dog." I didn't consider them a threat, so I warned them. I said, "You'll end up in a wooden overcoat if you trouble us, boys." They laughed at me. I gave them one last chance to walk away, but they didn't stop laughing and said, "You don't have Martin with you to back you up, bitch." I replied, "I don't need Martin or anyone else for this."

They then prepared themselves for the fight and said, "Let's see what you've got, cake-eater." These kids had a sharp tongue that wounded my ego. I put on my knuckle dusters and began to beat them up like a rabid dog in the street. I broke every one of their mouths, especially the one who had made me angry. Eventually, they managed to help themselves escape from me. I knew they wouldn't cause trouble for my girl after that.

I thought Abigail would be impressed by my bravery, but she didn't praise me. Instead, she simply thanked me with a tight hug. I consoled myself and gave her the locket. She asked, "Why did you give me a locket instead of a chain, Ethan?" I replied, "It's a self-defense locket, Abe. Pull it." She opened it and found sharp edges, and I told her to use it when necessary. I promised her that I would always be there for her before she needed to use it. She was touched by my promise and hugged me once more before entering her home and saying, "Good night, Ethan."

CHAPTER FOURTEEN

PILLAR BREAK

I woke up late that morning, even my mom hadn't woken up yet. When I finally woke up, it was already 9 a.m. so I got ready as quickly as possible and grabbed a sandwich to eat while driving. By 10 a.m., I reached Master's Villa and hurried to the meeting room where Nicholas was standing in front of the door. When he saw me, he asked me to come quickly.

I entered the meeting room and saw lots of photos and papers on the table. Sam and Danny also seemed clueless about the photos and files. Master then asked me to take a seat. Everyone in the room looked tense, but I wasn't sure why they were so serious about the photos and files on the table. I guessed that these items were brought by Anderson. Seeing our confusion, Master asked Sam to give the photos to Anderson. He then asked Anderson to explain about the photos. Anderson took a water bottle and drank from it before beginning to talk.

Anderson started, "Please pay attention, young men. This is a serious mission. You know that we had planned to undermine the support of Joseph [who has passed]. It's time, buddies. He is hosting a party for his policemen at a beach house tomorrow. Only police personnel will attend, no public, no friends, no politicians, but lots and lots of imported pussies. Our target, however, is only the policemen. So, we should not harm any other people. Do you understand?" I said, "Yes, but what's the plan?" To which he replied, "We are going to plant a bomb in the theatre on the 3rd floor of Joseph's beach house." Danny was surprised to hear that Joseph had a private theatre in a beach house. Anderson continued, "In that theatre, he is going to give a speech to his police dogs." Sam asked, "How can you say he will give the speech at the theatre only? He has a beach house, so he may give a speech on the shore too, right?" Anderson replied, "It is not safe for him, Sam. That's why he is going to give the speech in the theatre, as it is the only place where more than 300 people can sit. He will arrive at 9:30 a.m. and leave by 9:50 a.m. It will be heavily guarded. Sometimes Joseph will not attend the party, so he will send his accountant, Mr. Jeremy, to convey his words to them. If Joseph does come, we are going to hit the jackpot by blasting him, or else we will blast his men and his accountant. In this task, we are not going to kill anyone other than the police or Joseph's men. When they are in the theatre, all servants are kicked out of the house for security protocol." Danny asked, "What about the girls?" Anderson replied, "Bitches will only come in the evening, you dickhead." Sam asked for the plan to enter.

So, Anderson said, "You are going in as a cleaner. (Sam, Danny, and I were in shock.) Look, in this party, all work is split up and given to separate contractors, but we have a friendly relationship with Pearl Shine Cleaning Service, so they will send you as the cleaner and provide you with brand new ID cards." Sam was not happy to hear that. He refused to be part of the mission, but Master ordered him to participate. Eventually, he agreed to go as a cleaner.

Anderson continued his explanation, saying, "Yes, you are going to enter as a cleaner. You must act like cleaners. Acting is crucial in this mission, my boys, as it will disguise you from the guards. Once inside, you should enter the theater. I have already mentioned that the cleaning service will assist you in gaining access to the theater. They informed me that while the cleaners are cleaning the seats and stage, at least five armed guards will be monitoring them. Therefore, you must plant the bomb without being detected."

The plan looked clean and perfect, but the problem was the bomb. I was worried about carrying the bomb inside the beach house and the theatre because it was impossible. So, I asked Anderson, "What about the bomb? How are we going to take that in?" For that, he said, "You are not going to take that in. You are going to take the bomb from there only." (Sam, Danny, and I were in shock.) Yes, it's impossible to take the bomb in with us. There is an armory on the second floor where you can take the explosive. The armory was guarded by two armed guards. Inside the beach house, they don't check you, but if you seem suspicious to them, they will check you. Inside the armory, only one guard will be there to monitor you, and one more thing, only one cleaner is allowed to enter the armory." We felt it was a risky thing because there were many chances to get caught. So, I said, "This plan has many holes. We three don't have any experience in setting bombs. It's not like throwing dynamites at a crocodile, so we need a bomb expert with us." Anderson was quite heated by my opinion and opposition, so he criticized me and my brothers as "unskilled dicks," which even made Master tense. So, he asked Anderson to shut his mouth and said to me that he would arrange for a bomb expert and said, "Ethan, you mentioned the holes in the plan. So, I think you can sketch a plan for this mission. Is it okay for you?" I took a minute to sketch a plan and said, "Sure, Master. I have a plan." Then Master asked me to explain the same.

I took a deep breath and said, "Okay, here is the plan. First, we will enter the beach house as cleaners from Pearl Shine cleaning service. Then, I'll hide in the trolley of the cleaner, which will be pulled by the bomb expert to the armory. Inside the armory, I'll take care of the guard. The bomb expert will handle the explosives and set a timer on it. Finally, the bomb will be given to me. They will then exit the armory the same way they entered. After that, Sam, Danny, and the bomb expert should go to the third-floor washroom individually to collect their bombs. The bomb expert and I will enter first, then leave the trolley and exit. The remaining two will then enter and collect the rest.

Once we have all the bombs, we will move to the theater to plant them. That's the plan." Everyone in the room agreed with my plan except for Anderson. Master was very impressed with my plan and said, "Well planned, Ethan. I will arrange for the bomb expert. Take some rest. Tomorrow at 6:30 AM, you should be there. Keep in mind that some of them may recognize you, so keep a low profile. Is that clear?" We responded, "Clear, Master." Then we went home to rest.

It was January 8, 1931. I woke up early in the morning to prepare for my mission. At 5:30 AM, the Pearl Shine cleaning service van arrived at my house. I boarded the van where Sam and Danny were already dressed in their cleaner uniforms. They handed me a uniform, which I put on. In the van, I saw a middle-aged man who introduced himself as a bomb expert hired by Master. As I was about to explain the plan, he stopped me and said that Master had already briefed him. After an hour, we finally arrived at the beach house, which was heavily guarded. The van was stopped, and the guards instructed us to get out. Sam, Danny and I were scared of being caught by the guards, so they prayed to God to save us. Their prayers were answered as we were able to escape without being recognized by the guards.

Once inside the beach house, we began to execute our plan. Everything was carried out flawlessly. Eventually, we reached the theatre with bombs in our trolley. There were around ten guards in the theatre, but we managed to plant the bomb without being detected. After 15 minutes, the guards asked us to leave the premises. We moved to the shore, where the other servants were waiting. We waited for the right time to escape from the area, checking our wristwatches frequently.

Finally, many cars entered the beach house and a rich woman came out from the middle car, followed by a man. However, they were not clearly visible to us, so we used the small binoculars to try and identify the man. Unfortunately, it turned out to be Mr. Jeremy and his personal whore. They entered the house with guards, prompting us to decide to escape the area undetected. We sneaked to our van, changed our clothes, and waited for the explosion. Eventually, the bomb that we had planted went off, causing half of the building to collapse.

After the explosion, Sam drove the van quickly back to our place. I was hidden in the back of the van, but the Iron gang members somehow found us and started to chase us. Many cars were chasing us and firing bullets at us. I asked Sam and Danny for a gun, but we hadn't brought any big weapons, so Sam instructed me to manage with my pistol. We managed to stop five cars by shooting the drivers, but there were still more chasing us. Suddenly, my gun ran out of ammo, forcing me to hide my entire body under the seat to avoid getting hit. It was the roughest ride of my life, but suddenly two cars came close to us, and two Iron gang members jumped into the back of the van where I was hiding. We fought, and they tried to shoot me, but I managed to kick their pistols out of the van. We then engaged in a knife fight where I ended up killing both of them by slitting their throats. Unfortunately, they fell on top of me, causing me to lose my balance and fall hard on the floor, hitting my head. I was knocked unconscious.

CHAPTER FIFTEEN

MARRY ME

I didn't know what happened next. Then I felt cold water sprinkling on my face, and I opened my eyes. It was Sam. He helped me to get up and open the back door of the van. It was dark outside and all my visions were blurred. I couldn't see properly. I looked at my watch, and it showed around 8:00 p.m. Then I asked Sam, "What the hell happened? Did we accomplish our mission?" He replied, "Yes, buddy. We made it. But it was tough. They didn't stop chasing us. They kept coming with guns. We thought you were dead, but fortunately, you're not, man."

I felt tired, so I asked for water. Danny gave me a bottle of water, and I drank it. After drinking it, my vision improved. I realized that I was in the backyard of Master's Villa. I sat on the floor and tried to regain my energy. Then I said, "Damn, it feels like a hangover. Okay, I'm going home. Good job, buddy. Good night." I stood up to walk, but Sam said, "Aunt Margaret is here, Ethan. She and my mom are preparing cakes for tomorrow's church service. She's staying here tonight." So, I said, "I'm going inside to have some cake." But Sam stopped me. I was clueless about what he was doing, so I asked him the same. He pointed out my blood-soaked suit and said, "Look at your suit. It's dripping blood, Ethan. Your suit soaked up litres of blood from those two assholes. If you go inside like this, your mom will definitely faint. So go home. Aunt might prepare dinner for you."

I checked my long suit for blood, but I didn't find any blood stains. Sam then asked me to squeeze the suit with my hands, and I did the same. I was shocked to see blood dripping from my suit. I accepted Sam's decision and said, "Fine, I will finish my dinner at Uncle George's restaurant and then go home." However, Danny informed me that Uncle George was out of town and Abigail had closed the restaurant 30 minutes earlier, suggesting I go straight home. I was frustrated to receive this news, as it left me with no other options.

After calming myself down, I bid Sam and Danny good night and left the place. Suddenly, I remembered that the bomb expert was not with Sam and Danny, so I inquired about his whereabouts. Sam, annoyed, replied, "Ethan... He is safe at home, buddy. You're talking like a drunk idiot. Just go home." With that, I left the area.

Since I had not taken my car that day, I decided to walk home. It was a chilly night with a clear sky and no stars in sight, indicating rain. I picked up the pace, but before long, it started to rain. Walking down the street, which was a shortcut to my home and Abigail's house, I came up with a plan. Then I decided to use the rain as an excuse and ran to Abigail's house. I knocked on the door three times, but she did not respond.

I was a little nervous at that time because I feared that she might think badly of me, but I managed to push through my fear and knocked on the door three times again. This time, she responded to my knock. She said, "Wait," and I was so happy to hear her voice in that chilly weather. I heard her footsteps, and then she opened the door.

She looked stunning. It felt like a movie scene, but it was happening in my life. She was wearing a lavender-colored short frock with white dots on it. For the first time, I saw her without footwear, and her feet looked as soft as a wedding cake. I noticed sweat drops on her forehead, neck, and chest. She was also sexy. I saw a sweat drop from her forehead trickle down to her chest, disappearing into her cleavage. She noticed that my eyes were not meeting hers and asked, "Ethan, what happened? Come inside. I'll bring you a towel." Then she took my right hand and pulled me inside. She asked me to stand on the doormat so that the water dripping from my suit wouldn't dirty the floor. She went into her room and threw a towel at me from there, but I didn't want to dirty it with blood, so I just held onto it.

Then she brought me a shirt and pants belonging to Uncle George for me to wear. When she saw me, she asked, "What happened to you, Ethan? Dry yourself." She walked towards me and said, "Give it to me. I'll dry your hair." But I stopped her because I felt guilty for having her in my life and my heart. I thought that I didn't deserve such a sweetheart and godly angel in my life.

So, I said, "Look, Abe. You know me. You know what I am. You know what I do for a living. I know that you also have feelings for me. But I don't think that I deserve you. I am a killer, a mercenary, a hired gun. I am not fit for a family and I am a curse. I killed my father and mother. I don't know when I am going to die. Literally, I am counting my days, Abe. My hands are stained with blood. I am a sinner." But suddenly, Abigail threw a sofa cushion at me and ran to me. She hugged me tightly. She noticed something sticky on her cheeks and hands. She smelled me and found that the dripping from my suit was not rainwater, but blood. She saw that her cheeks and hands had impressions of blood from my suit. But she once again hugged me tightly and said, "You are mine, Ethan. I don't worry about your job. I want you to be a good man, a good husband, and a good father. That's it."

I was emotional at that time to see a person who loved me more than anyone. So, without thinking further, I said, "Marry me, Abe." She didn't take a second to think and said, "Okay." Then we kissed for the first time. It was the sweetest memory in my life as her lips.

CHAPTER SIXTEEN

LITTLE MERCY

Months passed. I enjoyed those taskless days with my Abe. We had a lot of fun rides in my car, exchanged infinite kisses, and had unforgettable sex. However, after a few months, Master had a task for us.

As usual, I went to Master's Villa and entered the meeting room where Master, Anderson, and Mr. Nicholas were present. However, Sam and Danny were not there, and we didn't know the reason. We waited for some time, but we lost hope that they would come. So, The Master asked me to convey the task to them when I saw them both, and we started the meeting.

Then the Master began to initiate the meeting and said, "We have successfully broken the police support of Joseph. This is a key step in weakening Joseph's business. Congratulations on that. However, we are not finished yet. As we all know, one of Joseph's main businesses is prostitution. There are four main brothels in Moonshine that are part of Joseph's prostitution ring. One is located at the border of Moonshine, one near the beach house that we destroyed, one near the warehouse on Lady Roth Street, and finally one near the Barrett's house. All of these brothels share the same name, KITTY SHOP.

So, what you guys are going to do is blast these brothels. Anderson will also accompany you. Our task is to dismantle the brothels. When you enter the brothel, you won't have much time as they are heavily guarded by Joseph's men. Save as many girls as you can, but do not forget the main task. Ethan, Anderson, Sam, and Danny will lead the team of eight. They are talented and skilled gunners, so there is no need to worry about them.

Anderson, you will take care of the brothel outside of Moonshine. Ethan, you will handle Lady Roth Street. Sam and Danny, you will take care of the beach house and warehouse brothels. Are we clear?" [We nodded our heads] "Then begin your task, boys. Go to the garage and pick up a van for you and your team. In the van, you will find the remote bomb that will be used for the beach house blast. Your teammates will arrive shortly. Get moving, boys. Good luck. I expect everyone to be back in my meeting room tomorrow."

I nodded my head and left the Villa, heading towards the garage where I saw Sam and Danny. I didn't know why they were standing there without attending the meeting inside, so I went to them and asked about the reason. They were very worried, as their hands were shaking. I asked them to tell me what happened and to explain the reason for their worries. For a while, they hesitated to share their concerns, but eventually, they were ready to open up.

Sam began to say, "Ethan, I don't know how you are going to take this. But please forgive me and help me with this, brother." I was clueless about what he was talking about, so I asked, "What the hell are you talking about, Sam? Make it clear." Sam then said, "We are in trouble, Ethan. Master is going to kill us." I forced them to tell me the matter clearly once again. Then he said, "We know what Master said in the meeting room." I was surprised and asked, "How?" Sam said, "Yesterday Danny snuck into Master's room and got the file. I know that you are going to take down the brothel on Lady Roth Street. I know that Master asked us to bring the prostitutes safely to our territory." I interrupted him and asked, "What is in it, Sam? It's Master's order." He replied, "I know that, Ethan. But... okay. Me and Danny used to go to Lady Roth brothel, and there is no problem with Danny, but with me. For the past year, we have been going there. I have a favorite woman, Mia. She doesn't know me as a Mechanic or as Master Martin's son. I used to harm her by whipping her in the breasts. Many times, I tortured her during sex. Once she became pregnant by me, and I killed the fetus by kicking her in the stomach. I thought she would die in pain, but she did not. Yesterday, I went there, but she refused to cooperate with me. She was furious with me and tried to attack me, but I beat her up. And now you are going to bring her to our home. If she comes to our place, it's impossible to stop her from complain me to my father. So please help me with this, Ethan. Please."

I was not at all expecting this from them and I decided not to help them, but I asked him to tell me how I could help. He said, "Ethan, please kill her and let her blast with the building." I was speechless and shocked by his inhuman thoughts, but I had a fear that if I didn't kill her, he would definitely kill her in the future. So, I thought for a minute and then I said, "Okay, Sam. I will do it for you." He jumped on me and hugged me tightly. He said, "Thanks a lot, my brother. I won't forget this, and please don't tell this to Master." I nodded my head and got into my van.

But I didn't plan to kill Mia. I had planned to send her to a safe place away from Sam so that she could live safely.

But if I told this to Sam, he would kill her. Then I started the van and went to the brothel on Lady Roth Street. I knew what I was going to do, so I took a breath and recollected everything that had happened that day. Then I asked everyone in the van to exit and ordered them to kill every Joseph man in the building.

I exited the van and walked to the building. There was no one at the counter, so I took all the cash. My team was on a killing spree, killing nearly every man in the brothel. Then I asked some of the girls on the ground floor about Mia, but nobody knew her. So, I moved to the first floor, where I knocked on every door and asked for Mia, but received negative responses. I then knocked on room number 8 but it wasn't opened or responded to. I kicked open the door and saw an old man trying to undress a girl in lingerie. I shot the old man and asked the girl for her name. She was shocked and scared after witnessing a live murder and urinated in her panties, which were soaked with blood. She hesitantly said, "Mary Richard." I asked if she knew Mia, to which she replied, "It's me. That's the name given to me by the pimp."

I was relieved to have found her and said, "Thank God, Mia. This is not a safe place for you. Do you know Sam? (She nodded with anger and fear in her eyes.) Yes, he is a member of the Mechanic gang like me and he is Master Martin's son. The Master sent us to protect all the girls here and bring you back to our town. However, Sam is not happy about it because he fears you will expose the truth about him to the Master. He sent me to kill you, but I refuse to do so."

Mia didn't trust me and refused to believe what I was saying. Despite my efforts to convince her, she remained skeptical. I could see the pain and lack of trust she had experienced over the years. I approached her, but she moved away until I hugged her tightly, making it difficult for her to escape. She was weak and vulnerable at that moment. She cried loudly. She loosened up her bra and showed me her breast, which had a cigarette mark. She showed her breast to me in the thought of her client, which made me cry too. I told her that I was not there for sex, but to take her to a safe place. I retrieved her dress from under the bed and gave it to her, then asked her to wear it. I gave her all the cash that I had taken from the counter, which was a considerable amount. I asked her to move to a safer place. She was very afraid. She told me she was an orphan and born in that brothel. I wanted to help her, so I suggested her to go to Uncle George's restaurant. She took the money and ran for her freedom. I decided to monitor her regularly and then I exited the room and shouted, "Has everyone evacuated the building?" One of my team members came to me and said, "All clear, Ethan. Ready to set the fire." I instructed them to set the timer and exit the building. Then I exited the building. I waited for them. They came one by one to the van and gave me the fuse to blast the building. I set the fuse on fire and entered the van. Then I drove the van and heard the blast sound behind me. Every Mechanic in the back was celebrating the accomplishment of our task. We then reached Master's Villa and waited for a few more minutes. Later, Sam arrived at the Villa. He opened the door and ran to me to ask about Mia. I said, "She is dead, Sam," which made him jump for joy. That night, I met Mia with Uncle George. He said that he was going to drop her off at his village, where Abigail lived.

CHAPTER SEVENTEEN

THE FIRE AND FURY

Months passed. Many gang wars occurred; many strategies were planned. Many were successful, but some hit us from behind. Abe became my life and wife in my heart. Few fights but lots of love.

One day, I was sleeping in my bed around 1:30 p.m. I was very tired and sick that day. My mom and Abe told me to rest without going anywhere, and I followed the same. My mom took care of me like a baby. She fed me. I enjoyed being a kid again, but suddenly at 1:30 p.m., I heard a horn sound. I didn't pay attention and thought the horn sound came from my dream, but it did not. So, I got up and looked through the window. I saw a car that seemed familiar, but I didn't see it properly. I opened the door and walked to the car. I was shocked because it was Master Martin. When I reached him, his eyes were red and shedding silent tears. I was helpless at that time and asked him to come with me to my home. At first, he refused. Then I forced him to come with me. I made him sit at the dining table and asked him, "Did you eat your dinner, Master?" He said, "I am dead, my son. Corpses don't need food." Then I understood that he was on an empty stomach. So, I took the cereal packet and a bottle of milk, mixed them in a bowl, and asked him to eat. But he didn't even touch the bowl. I understood that he was not willing to go to the house and he was mentally affected. I asked him the reason for his worries as he did not seem to be normal. I wanted him to share his worries with me, so I tried my best to get him to open up. Initially, he did not tell me about his worries, but eventually, he began to talk.

Master said, "Like others think, I didn't hate my brother, Joseph. I know he is a pain, but he is my brother. I used to post letters thrice a year to Joseph, but I didn't receive a single reply. However, I didn't stop sending my posts because I wanted to rebuild the family. Yesterday, when I was in my room, a pile of posts was on my table. It's a usual thing because I receive many posts a day. So, I opened them one by one and noticed a post from someone named Joseph. I wasn't excited to see the name Joseph since I had received many posts from that name before. When I opened it and read it, it was from my brother, Joseph. In the post, he apologized to me for the trouble he had caused and asked to meet me at Melody Bar at 6:00 p.m. So, I went there alone at 5:50 p.m., but he didn't show up for the next two hours. Finally, he arrived at 8:30 p.m. When he saw me, he laughed and said, 'You family cocksucker. I killed your father, but you are trying to rejoin me in your family.' I was unable to digest the fact that he had killed my father and I burst into tears. I left the bar without saying a word. I want Joseph to be killed, but I don't want to be the one to do it."

I did not expect that from Master. We thought that he was waiting for the right time to finish off Joseph, but he did not think of that and went to the extreme to try to rejoin the relationship. I was glad to know the truth behind his father's death, so I told him to arrange a meeting tomorrow and sketch a plan to kill Joseph. However, he did not seem to accept my plan and said, "I want to kill him now." I was surprised and told him, "How can we go without a plan, Master? It is suicide. Wait until tomorrow. Then we can plan about it." But he did not accept it at all. I told him, "Master, we do not even know where he is. He may be in his house or in his professional space." He remained silent. I knew that his silence was a sign of unacceptance. So, I said, "We are already planning to kill Joseph, his business, and his family. We have already cut off his brothel houses. Next, it's his warehouses, his family, and finally Joseph. We have completed past missions without leaving any evidence of our involvement. We are in a good position already. If we rush, we will face huge gang wars. First, let us break all his pillars and then Joseph. Keep your patience, Master. Your patience is very important now." I knew that my speech would make him think about it. He thought a lot and finally decided to wait for the right time.

I was very happy with his decision. He then took the bowl of cereal to eat. I waited until he finished the bowl, then he stood up and hugged me. He said, "Thank you, my son. I am already late. I have to go home." Then he walked to his car and said, "You are Benjamin James, Ethan." He entered his car and drove to his house. So, I went to my bed and slept.

Days passed like lightning. It was 1932. On a fine day, as usual, we had our meeting. Initially, Sam, Danny and I waited outside because Master was talking to police officials. After 45 minutes, the door opened and nearly 20 policemen came out. Mr. Nicholas then called us in. We entered the room, but Anderson was not there. Sam asked for Anderson, to which Mr. Nicholas replied, "He will come tomorrow." The meeting then began. Master started by giving sweets to all of us. When we asked for the reason, he told us to wait and began to speak.

Master said, "I am very proud of you, Ethan, Sam, and Danny. You boys are the supporting pillars of me and the Mechanics. You destroyed half of Joseph's support, cut off police support, and ruined his prostitution business. Thanks to you, many girls have been rehabilitated in our town, and almost every girl from other states and countries has been sent back home. But your job is not finished yet. We now plan to ruin Joseph's warehouses too." I didn't react because blood and blasts have become a part of my life, so I didn't feel excited or afraid. Then he said, "So, I am making it clear that this is not a stealth mission." We are in shock because if we do not approach our task like a snake, it will be painful for us and the entire Mechanics. The police will protect us legally when we leave no evidence at the crime scene, but if we leave a single piece of evidence, they will not help us with that particular mission. So, Danny asked, "How will that be possible? Cops are not going to help us when we enter with attention." Then Master replied, "That's right, but I have talked to our cops about this unstealthy mission and we are not going to cover this up."

We are in total confusion and have no idea what we are going to do. So, I asked Master about the plan. He said, "It's very simple. We are not only going to destroy his business, but also his name, power, and reputation. You are going to do this in broad daylight. You will be well-armored and enter through the main gate, but don't worry, you are not going alone. Almost 50 Mechanics are coming with you, all of whom are well-trained and skilled. It should be a surprise for Joseph and his men. So, through the main gate, you should enter the warehouse. After that, Sam and Danny should throw Molotov cocktails at all the warehouses, with a company of four cars, and then exit the place with pride." Sam and Danny were jumping for joy. They were excited to show themselves off to the public. Master said that the plan would be executed the next day, so he asked us to prepare both mentally and physically for the battle. I then went to Abe and had a great time with her before heading home to rest.

The next day, I went to Master's Villa, where I saw a huge crowd in the backyard with auto and semi-automatic guns. Sam walked over to me and said, "You are late, my friend. Come and pick your gun." I chose the MG15 and Sam commented, "Nice pick, Ethan. It will suit you." Master then arrived and said, "Listen, boys. It's a very important day for us. It will decide the future of the Mechanics and the Iron gang. I want everyone to return safely to their homes. Keep that in mind. It's an unsounded war. Get to your cars and complete your tasks." We then ran to our cars, with Sam, Danny, and another Mechanic named Henry as my teammates and I drove to the warehouse.

All the cars followed a truck that was first in line. We left the truck to break through the main gate. We were the fifth car among fifteen. When the truck hit the gate, it crashed to the ground. We entered the warehouse and targeted the storage areas of each section. We threw Molotov cocktails into the warehouse to set it on fire. The men who were shooting at us ran in fear of the fire. After five minutes, the entire area was engulfed in flames, and the Mechanics killed every Iron gang member without leaving one for me. I didn't use my MG15, but I killed many using the Molotov cocktails. When the buildings caught fire, every Mechanic shouted a victory sound and got into their cars. Then we drove back to Master's Villa.

Each Mechanic involved in that mission is safe and rewarded with huge cash and gold-filled bags. Master was in a state of joy and danced with every Mechanic in the backyard. Then he called me and said, "I have lost my fear of the future of Mechanics because you are here, my son." He then informed me that my rewards had already been sent to my home along with my brand new "Red Bugatti Royale." I was so happy to receive that reward and went home in excitement to see the car.

When I saw the beast in front of my home, I felt like it was calling me for a drive. I asked my mom to sit in the passenger seat and we flew at top speed. My mom also enjoyed the ride. Then I went to Abe's house and picked her up in my new car. We went to Eve's Mountain and had a lusty night in the new car.

CHAPTER EIGHTEEN

ETHAN WEDS ABIGAIL

Every Mechanic is celebrating the scenario of powerless Joseph, but we didn't stop spying and monitoring Joseph's territory. At the same time, we also enhanced the safety of our territory. It was August 12. It was memorable because for the first time, Abe woke me up in my home. I was surprised to hear the voice of my girl in my room. At the same time, I thought that some problem must have happened, which is why she came to my home. But when I opened my eyes, I didn't see any sadness or worries on her face or in her eyes. She looked so beautiful that day with her happy lips. She wore a green short frock and looked so beautiful and tempting. So, I grabbed her left hand and pulled her to me. She fell on me, and her nose touched my lips. I kissed her nose. Then she stood up and hit me on my hand. I enjoyed the moment she was in my room. I stood up and tried to grab her waist, but she ran away from me in my room. When I was about to grab her, she stopped me and said, "My father and Uncle Martin are in your home, Ethan."

It was another surprise for me because the master came to my home only during some festival time, but Uncle

George came to my home for the first time. So, I was about to step down to the living room to pay a visit to them. But Abe stopped me and asked me to take a bath first. I tried to convince her to take a bath after talking to them, but she was very stubborn in her decision. So, she pushed me into the bathroom and threw a towel at me.

When I came out of the bathroom after bathing, she was still in my room with the grey pants and white shirt in her hands. I got close to her and kissed her on the lips, then grabbed her butt, but she hit my hands and told me to dress up. As she said, I dressed up according to her selection. She loved that outfit and said, "You look good, Baby." I thanked her and asked her the reason for the arrival of Master, Uncle George, and Abigail. She asked me to sit next to her, then she stood up and sat on my lap. It was so romantic. I kissed her cheek and asked the same question. Then she began to talk.

Abigail said, "Ethan, we are going to marry soon." I was shocked to hear that because I thought our marriage would happen three or four years later. I didn't know why she was saying that, so I said, "Why are you in a hurry, darling? We have time. We have age. We have money. We have tons and tons of love for each other. Let us enjoy our youth." [My hands slowly rubbing her soft thighs] "Don't rush, sweetheart. Just wait for two to three years, then we'll marry. But we are already experiencing married life." [I touched her panties and tried to pull them down]

She took my hands out of her panties and looked at me. Then she said sarcastically, "Oh. That's fine, Ethan. It will be nice too because in our wedding photos, you, me and our daughter are going to be so cute and lovely." I was shocked to hear that and words were not coming out of my mouth. She understood my condition and what I was trying to say.

So, she replied, "Yes, darling. I am carrying our baby in my womb. I checked with the doctor and she said that I am pregnant for one month. Yesterday I felt tired and fainted in the church. Aunt Margaret took me to the hospital. Then only we came to know that I am pregnant. She told me to bring my father to your home today and promised to hide from my father the fact that I am pregnant. I think she invited Uncle Martin to your home today because I was surprised to see Uncle Martin in your home. And one more thing. DON'T BLABBER ABOUT MY PREGNANCY TO YOUR UNCLE. Okay?" I said, "Okay" in confusion.

I was still in shock to bear the truth that we were going to have a child but I did not understand the reason why she addressed our baby as "SHE". So, I asked the same question to her. For that, she said, "I know it, Ethan. Our baby is a girl. My guess won't be wrong, my future husband." Then she laughed but I did not even smile at her. She asked about my worries. So, I said, "I am happy that we are going to have a girl baby but will our marriage happen smoothly without any problems?" Abe was tense and irritated by my unnecessary fears. She said, "Ethan, you're already accepted by my father as a son-in-law. Then why are you feeling bad about it? For our marriage, money won't be a problem because you and I have plenty of it. So what? Let's get married." I said, "Okay" and hugged her from behind. She then took my hands and kissed them. A few minutes later, she asked me to go and talk to them.

Following her instructions, I went to the living room. When Uncle George saw me, he stood up and walked over to me, giving me a tight hug. He said, "We have decided to arrange a marriage for you and my daughter on September 3. Is that date okay for you, my son?" I was thrilled to see him so joyful about the wedding date because September

3 was Abigail's birthday. So, I said, "I am glad to marry Abigail and expand my family with you, Uncle George." Master clapped his hands out of extreme joy and said, "Finally, my kids are getting married to their loved ones. The full wedding expense is on me. Every bit of my kids' weddings will be paid for by me. Your only job is to select nice outfits for yourselves, that's it." He stood up and hugged me with love. I was so happy to receive so much love that morning. My mom came to me and said, "Finally, my son is going to become a family man. I am very happy, Ethan." She whispered in my ear, "Take care of my two girls." Then she kissed my cheek. It was the happiest day for me. I saw Abe standing on the stairs, blushing beautifully as we talked about our wedding. Her eyes conveyed love for me.

It was our wedding day, and Master Martin's arrangements were astonishing. Our wedding took place on an island near our town's shore. It was a small island with colorful birds and was decorated in white and red. I was given a white suit with white pants and a red rose in my suit pocket. I eagerly awaited my girl's arrival. Finally, she came with her father, looking stunning in her wedding gown. She stood next to me, and I told her, "You look so beautiful, Abe." She replied, "You too, handsome." We held hands tightly before exchanging rings.

The priest then asked us to exchange rings and kisses. First, I put a ring on her soft finger, and then she placed a ring on mine. We kissed in front of 150 wedding guests, who clapped and cheered for us. Sam and Danny lifted us in joy. My wife and I spent the night on a ship floating between Moonshine and the island where we got married. It was a beautiful experience to sleep under the stars and moon, but my Abe looked more beautiful than them all.

CHAPTER NINETEEN

EMPTY BARREL

Abigail was nine months pregnant. She had taken very good care of our daughter from the moment she found out about the pregnancy. Yes, we knew that we were having a girl. It was Abe's intuition and wish. I too wished for a girl baby. I greatly enjoyed my married life. It was a peaceful nine months for us. We even bought baby dresses for our unborn baby. It may sound silly, but we enjoyed it. During her pregnancy, I spent a lot of time with her instead of working on my tasks.

It was May 5th, 1932. I went to Master's Villa at 11:30 a.m. I entered the meeting room with Sam and Danny. I asked Sam to marry a girl, but he refused and said he was not interested in marriage but wanted to enjoy life with girls. In the meeting room, the Master was not there. We waited for nearly 40 minutes, but Master and Nicholas did not arrive. Anderson came to the meeting and was also shocked by their absence. A few minutes later, we heard a screeching tire sound near the entrance gate. We ran to the spot with guns in case of an emergency. It turned out to be Master, who looked terrible because his white suit was now red with blood.

I ran to the car and was shocked by the scene. I screamed loudly, and upon hearing my scream, everyone in the Villa came to us. I was weeping because in Master's lap, Nicholas' head was there, and his body lay next to Master. Nicholas' blood was on Master's suit. Master's eyes were filled with tears. Nicholas was a very lovely and respectable man. His death was unbearable for us. Master took Nicholas' head in his left hand and lifted his body with his right hand. Sam, Danny, and I were crying on the floor. Master was not able to lift Nicholas, so we helped him lift Nicholas' body. Master didn't speak a single word. We asked him to tell us who was behind the death of Nicholas. Master said, "Barrett. It's Barrett. I saw him. Nicholas asked me to pick him up from the tailor shop by 11:30 a.m. I drove the car to that tailor shop. I saw Nicholas inside the shop, so I waited for him. Then he came. When he opened the co-pilot seat door, suddenly a car crossed us quickly. Then Nicholas' head landed on my lap. The people in the car cut off Nicholas' head. I saw Barrett and his men in the car."

After hearing this, we were left with no choice but to seek revenge. I said, "Barrett will die today, Master. He will... He will pay for Nicholas' death." Then Sam, Danny, and I took our guns and ammo with us. We promised everyone we would slit Barrett's throat. We got into a car and drove to the old gold mine, which was Barrett's resting place. More than 50 Mechanics followed us with guns to support us.

As we were heading to the old gold mine, we encountered four cars of Barrett's men chasing us. Sam was a better shooter than us. He shot three drivers and stopped the cars. Danny threw a grenade into the window of the fourth car, which exploded next to us and temporarily deafened us. We regrouped and discussed the plan for the chase. I said, "I don't think of it as a usual chase." Danny asked, "Then what are you thinking about it?" I replied, "It's a planned one, Danny. Someone informed that bastard about our plan. I think he may have even escaped from his place." Both of the brothers agreed with my opinion. Sam then asked me to drive as fast as I could, but I was already driving at maximum speed.

As we were almost reaching the old gold mine, we saw four cars speeding past us. Sam spotted the car and exclaimed, "Ethan, that's the bastard. He's escaping from us, man. Turn around, turn around." I turned my car and chased after him, giving full throttle. After a few minutes, I saw the cars entering the forest next to the road. It was Barrett. I turned the car and drove into the forest.

Sam instructed me to focus on Barrett's car and my driving. He assured me that he and Danny would take care of the men with their guns. Sam and Danny managed to shoot down all the cars except Barrett's. Barrett proved to be very elusive, dodging almost every bullet while driving. However, Sam and Danny made him to hit a tree with his car. Barrett's car began to emit smoke from the engine, but he got out and took cover behind it. We also took cover behind our car. We were unable to penetrate Barrett's body with our bullets, so I threw a grenade under his car. The explosion shattered his car's windows into a thousand pieces and produced a sudden cloud of black smoke from the engine. We used the smoke and approached him. I went behind Barrett and kicked the gun from his hand. He then took out a knife and tried to kill me, but Sam shot him in the hands and knees.

Barrett fell to the ground, and his blood was running in the muddy ground. He begged for his life, offered money and business deals to us, but we did not consider his offers.

He continued to negotiate, so I took my knife and cut off his tongue. Then I removed his shirt, cut it into pieces, rolled it into a ball, and used it to close his mouth. I asked Sam and Danny to lock him in the car boot. They locked him in the boot of our car.

Upon entering the villa, it remained as we had left it. Master was still mourning Nicholas' death, with his body and head on his lap. Aunt Sandra was present, appearing frightened. Danny went to take care of her. No one in the place had any idea of what we had done. Sam and I opened the boot and carried the man inside. We threw him to the ground, and everyone in the place began kicking him. I knew he had died after the fourth kick, which hit his neck. Master then instructed them to throw Barrett at Joseph's house entrance gate, after cutting his head and body separately.

Then, I went to my house and cried to my mom and Abe, but I controlled it because I didn't want them to be worried.

CHAPTER TWENTY

COLLAPSED ROOF

Nicholas memories weren't faded from my heart. He was a gem of a person. That night, I didn't sleep a bit. I made Abigail sleep instead of crying, but she didn't sleep. I made her lay on my lap and stopped her from weeping. She was not in her normal mind. I knew that she was thinking something else. I knew that she was thinking something related to our future. So, I asked her to tell me what she was thinking. She said, "Honey, shall we go somewhere else? We don't want to stay here. You, Aunt, Dad, and me. We will go somewhere and settle in safer place. A peaceful life. No blood, no murder, and no revenge. I don't want to raise our daughter here, Ethan. Please. Do this for me and your daughter." I didn't know what to tell her, but I felt that it was the absolute truth and a needed one because I didn't even prefer Moonstone as the place where my daughter to born and lived. So, I thought for few minutes and promised her to fulfil her wish, but I told her, "Sweetheart, we'll go to some nice place away from Moonshine. But I have things to do. You know that, right? Joseph...Arthur...that's all. Please, Abe. If I don't finish them off, they won't let us live a peaceful life." Abigail wasn't happy with my statement, but I somehow managed to calm her down.

Then, she slept on my lap, but I didn't sleep a bit. My heart was not stable because I knew that Joseph and the Bear wouldn't settle down without killing us. I thought a lot about it and tried to figure out a solution, but I was left with the death of Joseph and the Bear as a solution. I knew that Master also wouldn't be sleeping, so I was thinking of going to Master's Villa.

I lifted Abe's head and placed it on the pillow next to me without disturbing her sleep. I informed my mom about my visit to Master and asked her to sleep in my room. Then I took my car and went to Master's Villa. As I guessed, it was still filled with Mechanics. I went to the back where some doctors were doing something with Mr. Nicholas' body. When I saw Nicholas' dead body again, I started to weep. I was tapped on my shoulder. I turned to that person and it was Master. He said, "I know that you will come. Tomorrow at 9:30 AM is Nicholas' funeral. You know that." [I nodded my head] "Yeah... yeah... you knew it. The Ragnarok has started for us, Ethan. It's time to finish off the Iron gang's chapter. If not, we'll be killed by those bastards. Come, Ethan. They are waiting for you." Then I followed him to the meeting room where Sam, Danny, and Anderson were already there. Master made me sit and then he took a seat.

Everyone was in silence with grief over Nicholas' death. Danny was still weeping. The Master gave a water bottle to Danny and asked him to drink it. Danny then drank the entire bottle. The Master began to speak, saying, "It's a great loss. I lost my friend, a loyal accountant, manager. He was everything to me." He took a deep breath and continued, "Okay. I want to finish off this rival. I want that bear, Joseph, and his men to be dead within a week. But tomorrow, I want Arthur Morgan to be dead, then Joseph. There is no plan, it's an absolute, sound attack. Joseph knows that we'll come and he will be prepared for our arrival, but I don't care about it. I want the heads of Arthur and Joseph. Got it?" I replied, "Yes, Master." The Master then stood up and said, "For Nicholas," before heading to his room. After a few minutes, Anderson and I exited the villa. I then went to my home.

I entered my room where Abe and my mom were sleeping. I closed the door and lay on the sofa in the living room, but I didn't sleep. I was thinking about the missions we were assigned and Abigail's wish. I decided to fulfil both my missions and Abigail's wish. A few hours later, the window began to let in the rays of sunlight. I stood up and went to my room, where my mom was not there. She was in another room. I asked her to get ready for Nicholas' funeral. Then I woke up my girl and asked her to get herself ready. After 15 minutes, I bathed her because she found it difficult to do so on her own. Then I dressed her up. In the meantime, I took a bath and got ready. I took my car and went to Master's Villa with my mom and Abigail.

Master had decided to bury Nicholas in the backyard of his house. The gravedigger had already dug a pit for him. The priest was standing in front of Nicholas' body. We were in grief. Then the priest asked us to lift the coffin of Nicholas to the pit. Sam, Danny, Master, uncle George, Anderson, and I lifted Nicholas' coffin. Then we moved to the grave which was dug. The priest asked us to place the coffin inside the pit. He chanted for 10 minutes and asked the gravediggers to close the coffin by nailing it.

By 5 p.m., Sam, Danny, Master, Anderson, and I met in the meeting room to discuss the attack. Anderson said that, according to his intel, he had learned that Arthur was not in town and had escaped to another country. He also mentioned that Joseph was under full protection, with every man, including Arthur's men, guarding him in his house. Master insisted that we sketch a plan to take down both father and son. I felt it was a valid point. Master then gave us 12 hours to sketch a plan and, on the 18th hour, ordered us to execute it. We accepted his order, and then Master left the meeting room.

Sam, Danny Anderson, and I were staying in the meeting room. Sam asked Anderson, "Is your intel true, Anderson? Because I don't think Arthur is such a coward to run away." When Anderson heard that he was enraged and said, "Stop your words, fucker. I am more loyal than you. I have seen you in Joseph's brothel, you son of a bitch." Sam was also angry and went to knock him down, but we somehow managed to control them. A few minutes later, Sam told me, "It's already late, Ethan. Go to your home. Abigail will be waiting for you." So, I was about to leave the villa, but Anderson stopped me and asked me to stay there until the deaths of Arthur and Joseph. Sam was furious and went against Anderson's request, asking me to go home. As he said, I went home.

At my home, Uncle George and Aunt Sandra were there with my mom and Abigail. Uncle George and Aunt Sandra were convincing Abigail to be patient for a few more days. Then Aunt Sandra told me, "Ethan, it's your duty to care for these two women. They were born for you. This is not a suitable place for them, Ethan. Make arrangements for them. Leave Moonshine and live the rest of your life in a beautiful and peaceful place on Earth. Please, Ethan, do it for your child in her womb." She then hugged me and went home.

Abe was sitting on the couch. I went to her and sat at her feet. I took her left foot and gave it a massage. Then I took her hands and held them tightly. I made a promise to her. I said, "Sweetheart, look at me. You know how much I love you. You know that I would do anything for you. By tomorrow morning, we are moving to a new place. A temporary safe place. We will go to your old house where Mia is living now. Then, uncle will search for a new place. A permanent place for us. Is that okay with you, my moon?" She hugged and kissed me, then said, "Love you, Ethan. But I know that after you leave me at my old house, you will go for Joseph. But I am sure you will return." I felt blessed to have a partner like her. I asked her to pack everything for the next day's travel, then we went to our room and slept.

Around 3:30 a.m., we heard a huge explosion sound, the vibration of which was felt in my bed. Abigail and I woke up. I went to the balcony to check the explosion, and my mom, Uncle George and Abe accompanied me. We were shocked to see the explosion because it happened at Master's Villa.

CHAPTER TWENTY-ONE

SKINNED BEAR

I was screaming a lot. I couldn't tolerate the fact that the explosion had happened at Master's Villa. I didn't think positively. I thought that I had lost everyone in that explosion, including Master, Sam, Danny, and Aunt Sandra. I didn't think positively that they could be saved. I was shouting and screaming for my loss.

A few minutes later, I heard rapid gunshots from the direction where the blast had occurred at Master's Villa. I confirmed it was a surprise strike on us. I was both angry and consumed by grief at the same time. I was filled with rage, wanting to kill every member of the Iron gang with my gun.

I ran to my room and grabbed all my guns, loading them into my car. Abe, Mom, and Uncle George tried to stop me, but at that moment, I lost myself and was consumed by a monstrous rage. I was completely overshadowed by my inner monster. Abe was crying and tried to pull me back, but I didn't listen to her.

As I was loading the guns and ammo into my car, I heard Sam calling my name. I was surprised and felt happy to hear his voice. I turned around and saw Master's car, where Aunt Sandra, Sam, and Danny were seated. I was overjoyed to see that my family was alive. I asked about Master, but as I had feared, he was dead.

Aunt Sandra shouted, "Please, son, go away. It's not the right time to fight, Ethan. Look at your wife. She is pregnant. She is carrying a baby inside. You can't kill these bastards now. It's not the time. It's time to retreat, Ethan." Then she cried a lot. Abigail held my hands and said, "I beg you, Ethan. Come with me," and hugged me tightly.

It was complete chaos in our town. Many buildings were set on fire. Many people were running to save their lives. I saw many people who were badly injured and running for their lives. Some carried their family members who had already died. At that time, I felt like I had lost myself for a moment. I didn't even consider my girl's tears. I felt so bad and I snapped out of it. I kissed Abigail and said, "I'm so sorry, Abe." Sam asked us to make our way to a safe and secure place. After the search hunt was cleared by Iron gang, Sam asked to meet him at Eve's Mountain after sunset. Danny was crying over his father's death. I knew how much pain he was in. Then Sam said, "Look, brother. We are losing power temporarily. Every Mechanic is scattering to their safe place. But they will come for us. They know the protocol as you know. So, don't worry. We will win this war. But for now, get them to a safe place." [I nodded my head] "Good." [He hugged me] "Okay, be safe, brother. Abigail, be safe." Then he entered his car and asked Danny to drive, and they left.

In the meantime, Uncle George went to our house and picked up the luggage that had already been packed. He took the money bag with him, which was bigger than the others. Then he came out of the house, placed the bags on the ground, and listened to our conversation. When Sam arrived, he handed the luggage to me to arrange in the boot. I did so and then helped Abe get into the car. She held my hand and sat in the back passenger seat with my mom, while Uncle George sat in the co-pilot seat. It was a Mercedes Benz W15, which Abigail had given to me as a birthday gift. When she gave me the car, she said, "This charm will drive us to our dreamland, Ethan." At the time, I didn't understand Abigail's words, but now, everything was falling into place.

After everyone was on board, I drove quickly to our destination, Uncle George's old house where Mia was staying. We were about to leave our hometown but the BEAR seen us and started to chase after us. I had been expecting his arrival.

Arthur was on a killing spree, turning my town into ashes. He took a Tommy gun from one of his men in the passenger seat and began shooting at my car. For the first time, my hands were not steady while driving because I was afraid for my family's lives. I didn't want to lose them. When our car was hit, Uncle George put on his power glasses, took the Tommy gun, and fired back at Arthur.

I asked my mom and my girlfriend to cover their heads from the bullets. It was a medium-sized car, so Abe found it difficult to bend her head because her tummy was carrying our baby. My mom made her lay on her lap, and my mom laid on her hand. My mom held Abe's shoulder and stomach.

Uncle George was a sharpshooter when he was in service as a Mechanic. But I had doubts about him because of his age. He aimed the gun at the wheels and the drivers. Then he pulled the trigger. He was so accurate in his shooting that he killed the driver within a magazine. They were very close to us when the driver was killed. I saw through the rear-view mirror that Arthur opened the co-pilot seat door and kicked out the dead man from the car. Then Arthur took the driver's seat. He was very tall and looked like a giant. He handled a Tommy with one hand, holding the steering wheel with his right hand and the Tommy with his left hand. Then he began to fire. It was fully dark, and only the headlight helped me to drive. But suddenly, I drove through a hollow pit, causing everyone in the car to jump and hit their heads on the roof, including Abe. This made Abe scream in labor pain. I felt like a dead man. The moment she got her labor pain, she held my shoulder and screamed in pain. We didn't know what to do because we couldn't stop the car as Arthur was chasing us with a gun. I asked Uncle George to focus on his shooting because he had started to cry and had forgotten to defend us.

Unfortunately, Uncle George's power glasses fell on the road and were smashed by Arthur's car wheels, leaving him unable to see properly. As a result, he perked in the car, and I felt helpless and lost hope. However, Abe's screaming encouraged me to fight for life, so I drove the car as fast as I could. Arthur gained speed and came alongside me in his car. Seizing the opportunity, I took my pistol from my holster and shot him, penetrating his forearms and causing him to lose feeling in his hand. This led his hand to slide to the right, turning the steering wheel in that direction. Arthur's car sharply turned to the right and twisted on the road, providing me with a sense of relief as I took a deep breath.

I then had the chance to look at Abe, who was still screaming in labor pain. Her amniotic fluid protection was broken, and my mom informed me that she was about to give birth. Despite this, I could not stop the car as we could be found at any moment. My mom lifted Abe's skirt and removed her inner wear, revealing that her vagina was expanding and a tiny head was pushing from inside. The pain that Abigail was enduring was unbearable for me, so I turned my head to face the road. Abe asked me to hold her hands, so I reached back to give her my hands without turning around. She made a valiant effort to push out the baby, but it was not successful. After more than 20 minutes of trying to deliver the baby, she was unable to do so. At that point, I stopped the car, went back to Abe, and held her hands and head. But in fear, later, I closed her mouth with my hand because her screaming might attract enemies.

I still remember that day as if it were yesterday. My mom asked Uncle George to get outside the car. Then she spread Abigail's legs widely and asked her to place them on top of the co-pilot seat and driver's seat. The four of us were crying because of the pain that Abe was suffering. My mom asked me to keep a hand on her vagina so that when the baby came out, it would not get hurt. Abe tried her best but nothing happened. I made her lay her head on my shoulder and said, "Abe, take a breath, then try again." She tried that several times but on the final attempt, I felt a head coming out of her vagina. I asked her to push. She pushed and screamed loudly in pain. The next second, I had our baby in my hands. I was relieved. In the light of the lighter, I saw my newborn girl. She had the nose and eyes of her mom and she was so beautiful. The little sweetheart started to cry. Not only her, but everybody started to cry tears of joy. I gave her to Abe. She kissed her and held her close to her heart. Abe and I enjoyed the moment with our daughter. Meanwhile, my mom completed the remaining tasks. She cut the cord. Before our wedding, we had decided on the name of our daughter. We named her Olivia in my car. A few seconds later, my mom took Olivia and started to adore her. Then Uncle George came in and started to cry. He said, "Oh my Lord, you gave my mom to my daughter." Everyone was happy with the name of our daughter.

However, a sudden instinct told me that we were in danger of an Iron gang. So, I asked everyone to sit in their seats. Then I drove the car to our destination, driving it very smoothly at a medium pace. My mom asked Abe to breastfeed Olivia. I was so happy to be a father.

We were already two hours late. Everyone except Olivia was awake. My mom took a precautionary measure and tore a towel into two pieces to use as a diaper for Olivia. At 9 AM, the car stopped due to lack of fuel. Fortunately, Uncle George had brought 30 gallons of gasoline in the boot. So, we fuelled the car and started the journey again. Everyone was hungry, but we only had one loaf of bread. My mom split it into four pieces and gave it to us. I gave my share to Abe to eat. At first, she refused, but later took it out of compulsion. Around 12 noon, we reached our destination.

Mia came out of the house upon hearing the engine sound of the car. She ran to our car before we stopped and opened the back door. She was shocked to see a baby in Abigail's arms and helped her out of the car. Mia was jumping out of joy. Abe gave Olivia to Mia, who took her and kissed her on the forehead. She was very afraid to hold her, so she returned her to my mom. Abe told Mia Olivia's name, which she loved. Then she hugged and kissed Abigail on the cheek before coming to hug me. She stood on her toes and kissed my cheeks and said, "Thank you, Ethan." Mia was totally changed. She had gained weight, her wounds were gone, and she was much more socialized compared to our first meeting.

Then Mia held my hand and asked us to enter the house. The house was beautiful and decorated with paintings. Mia had a pet dog named Zeus, a pit bull. She made us sit on the sofa. Uncle George was stunned to see his own house because it was different from how he left it. Abigail said, "You made it a home, Mia." To which she replied, "It's all because of your paintings, Abigail. I took them from your room and decorated the house with flowers and plants." I was very shocked because she hadn't shared about her paintings, so I asked her about them. She replied, "At that time, I was alone. The paintings were my companions, but after you came into my life, I didn't feel the need for them anymore." I kissed her forehead and said, "I love you, Abe." Upon hearing this, George started to cry and apologized for making her suffer from loneliness. We somehow managed to calm him down and wipe away his tears.

Mia arranged the room for us and at 1 p.m. she called us for lunch. My mom also helped her make the lunch, which was delicious. After finishing lunch, I said, "It's time to go, Abe." However, everyone in the house stopped me and asked me to stay for at least a week to let the tense situation in Moonshine cool down. I saw this as a valid point, and the main reasons for my stay were my daughter and Abe.

CHAPTER TWENTY-TWO

BRAIN FLOATS

I enjoyed every moment with Olivia and Abe. We were a beautiful family. Olivia was accustomed to my warmth, and Abe was very happy that I was staying for a week. She kissed me in joy when I agreed to stay there. At that moment, everyone in the house forgot their problems and enjoyed the gathering. After lunch, everyone felt sleepy, so they went to their rooms to sleep. However, Abigail gave sleeping Olivia to my mom and came to me. She sat on my lap and said, "Ethan, I know you have to go. You are trying to solve every problem, but is it possible? Even if you take care of all the Iron gang members, the police won't let us live our lives. Think about our daughter, Ethan. She is safe now because they don't know about her, but they will soon. I don't know what to do, but we are still in trouble, Ethan." Then she lay on my chest and fell asleep. A few minutes later, I lifted her and put her on the bed, then I slept next to her.

In the evening, we went shopping in my car with everyone. We bought new dresses for everyone, including Olivia. Uncle George got new glasses. After shopping, we went for dinner. The food was average, but the time we spent together overshadowed the taste of the food. As we left the restaurant and got into my car, we heard rapid gunfire nearby. I was shocked to hear gunfire there, which I thought was safe. I knew that it was Iron Gang members. To confirm my doubts, I jumped out of my car, climbed the fire escape, and cleared my doubts. Yes, it was them. They were firing at Uncle George's house where we had spent the past five happy hours.

I was speechless because I didn't know what to do and how to safeguard my family. I climbed down and asked Uncle George to drive the car to a safe place. The car was already fully fuelled, so I asked him to go to a faraway place. Abe asked, "Then, you are not coming with us, right, Ethan?" I kissed her lips and said, "Within three to five days, I will meet you. It is a promise, Abe. You are a mother now. Take care of all of them." I then picked up Olivia and kissed her on the forehead. She was sleeping, but I said, "Bye, sweetheart. Daddy will come for you," then gave her back to Abe. I promised everyone my safe return. I asked Uncle George to drive safely and use the guns and money in the boot. I gave a Tommy gun and four 1911 pistols with ammo to Uncle George, Abigail, my mom, and Mia, and asked them to use them in case of a problem. I took a 1911 pistol with an extra magazine for myself. After a few minutes, I asked Uncle George to drive to a safe place. Abe was crying for me, but the car started moving. I, too, cried, but I had some jobs to do, so I wiped the tears from my hands and walked to Uncle's house.

There were eight men with Tommy, but I snuck up on them and surprised them with my bullets. I began my mission by shooting three of the bastards in the head, alerting the others to my presence. I took cover behind the wall of a saloon, which was already broken because of them, but managed to kill all of them. Afterward, I took a

Tommy gun and its magazines from them, as well as their car, which I drove to moonshine. After driving for three hours, the fuel tank ran empty. I refilled it with the fuel in the boot, but it wasn't enough. I resumed my journey but ran out of fuel again. Luckily, there was a gasoline station nearby where I pushed the car and filled the tank illegally. I continued my journey and finally reached moonshine. I then drove to Eve's mountain, hid the car in bushes, and waited for Sam. At 8 PM, Sam arrived and called out my name. I emerged from the bushes and Sam hugged me with joy.

Sam wept for the master's death and for losing control over the police. He revealed that Anderson was behind the chaos, having been sold to Joseph. Anderson informed them of our plan and planted a bomb in our home. He also gave sketches of our faces to the police, including our families. This news enraged me as I suspected Anderson of being a double agent. I said, "That bastard should be torn apart. His ribs should be broken into pieces." Sam promised me to do the same. He said that Anderson was staying in Joseph's house, so I asked about the plan. Sam replied, "It is a surprise attack, Ethan. But we have to wait until the 19th. Because all the Mechanics are scattered in different directions to protect their families, they will regroup by the 19th of May. After that, we can proceed with our plan alongside our brothers." I nodded and inquired about Danny and Aunt Sandra. Sam informed me that they were in a cave east of Eve Mountain. I asked Sam to take me there, and as promised, he led me to the cave where Danny and Aunt Sandra were waiting.

Aunt Sandra and Danny ran to me and embraced me when they saw me. They asked about me and my family, especially Abigail. I told them that I had become a father to a baby girl. They were delighted to hear the news and asked for her name. I replied, "OLIVIA," and they loved the name. We then had dinner in the cave, during which I recounted the events of the past days. They were deeply concerned about my family being alone without me. At midnight, we all settled down to sleep in the same cave to gather energy for our final task.

On the 19th of May, at 9:00 p.m., all the scattered Mechanics arrived at the cave, and our planning began. We had received information that Joseph and Anderson were at Joseph's casino, while Arthur Morgan was in the hospital. It was shocking to learn that Arthur was still alive but incapacitated. Sam somehow obtained the blueprint of the casino and showed it to all the Mechanics. The casino had multiple direct and indirect entrances. Therefore, I sketched out the plan and informed everyone in the cave. I said, "It is our final battle. We had already earned money for our next generation, so it will all be over when we have killed Joseph, Arthur, and Anderson. After that, we should split up and live as common men. Am I clear? (Everyone shouted, "Yes.") Good. We have more than 200 Mechanics here and 20 ways to enter the casino. There are four main entrances, each in a different direction, with the East gate entrance being the largest. Additionally, we have two sewage underground pipes and 14 air vents. Arthur is in the hospital, so Danny, you will take care of him with 10 Mechanics. I will lead the sewage underground pipe team and need a total of 40 Mechanics. Sam, you will lead the air vent team with 40 Mechanics. The rest will be in the main gate team. There is no leader in that team, but you are a vital part of my plan. Your job is to distract the guards and Iron gang by attacking them from the front gates. Do not worry, you will be given armor and machine guns. The casino has six floors, with VIPs and money holders on the ground and first floors only. The other floors will have politicians, actors, singers, and girls. I believe Joseph and Anderson will be on the fifth and sixth floors. That is the plan, Mechanics. Tomorrow at 4 AM, we will move to the casino and begin the battle. Take some rest and prepare your weapons. The main entrance team will receive their weapons and armor from Danny."

Then I asked everyone to disperse. I sat on the floor and started to think about my family but I convinced myself by saying that it was for my family. Aunt Sandra then asked me to sleep. As she said, I slept. Sam woke me up and asked me to gear up for the strike. Within five minutes, I geared up for the strike. I took a Tommy gun, a 1911 pistol, and four hand grenades with me. Then I went to my team. Before getting into the van, I asked Sam and Danny to be safe. I instructed Sam to kill the lights before entering the building. I boarded the van and reached the starting point of the sewage pipe, which was half a kilometer away from the casino. My team opened the lid and jumped into the pipe one by one. We began to walk inside. The moment we heard the firing sound, which came from the main entrance team, we climbed up and reached the parking lot of the casino. We opened the office room door in the parking lot and entered the ground floor of the casino where we saw more than 500 rich pigs. I aimed my gun at the roof and shot many bullets, causing everyone in the building to flee except the Iron gang members and casino guards.

We killed many guards and Iron gang members on the first floor. We collected ammo from the corpses. Then we climbed up to the first floor where I saw Sam and his team. We were doing well in our mission because almost every Iron gang member had been killed.

Sam and I, along with 20 Mechanics, searched for Joseph and Anderson on the 5th and 6th floors, and finally, we found them. First, we found Joseph in a room with a young girl who ran away with Joseph's money and watches. Sam shot him in the legs to immobilize him, and then I took a shotgun from one of the Mechanics. I inserted it into his mouth and pulled the trigger, causing Joseph's head to burst into pieces and half of his brain to fall on the floor. The room was covered in red from Joseph's blood, with flesh and brain pieces sliding down the walls. We then exited the room and searched for that police dog, finally finding him in the bathroom. Sam shot him in the legs and dragged him to the toilet, pressing Anderson's head into it. He then took the shotgun from me and shot Anderson in the head and back, filling the bathroom with his rip bones pieces. Sam felt relieved after killing Anderson. We then got into our van and went to Eve's mountain cave. We completed our job before the police arrived.

In the cave, we exchanged greetings and well-wishes for the future. Sam had a plan to move to Italy with Danny and Aunt Sandra on a cruise, which made me happy for them. I then left the cave, took the car, and drove to the uncle's town, where I had last seen them. Luckily, a restaurant owner informed me that they had left a letter for me. Then he gave the letter to me. I opened it. In the letter, Uncle wrote that they are moving to Alaska. Then the restaurant owner gave a bundle of money on behalf of Uncle George. I thanked the restaurant owner and drove to Alaska. When I reached half of the distance, the car broke down. I waited for another vehicle to come on the road. I waited nearly half a day, but finally, a truck came and helped me by dropping me off in Alaska.

Finally, I reached Alaska. I asked everyone about my family by describing their facial features, but I didn't find them. I lost hope and sat on the floor. After 20 minutes, I felt a touch on my shoulder. It was Uncle George. I hugged him, and he took me to where everyone was staying. I was so happy to see my family again. Abe was overjoyed and shed tears of happiness. She ran to me and hugged me. Then I saw my daughter in my mom's arms. Everyone was safe, and I felt relieved because I thought my journey had come to an end. However, that night we were caught by the police. I killed every police officer and escaped from the place with my family.

I was driving the car without knowing the destination. I was worried about my daughter's future. Abe was unable to stop her crying, but I managed to control her emotions and asked her to calm herself and the baby. I noticed that she was not in a normal state and knew that she was thinking of something else in her mind. I asked her to share her worries, but she said, "The chase will not stop, Ethan. We are going to suffer for our sins, but why should Olivia suffer? What sin did she commit? If she is with us, she will suffer pain as we are suffering. [She started to cry] Ethan, shall we leave Olivia with Mia? (Ethan gave a sigh of unacceptance) It's our only option, Ethan. Instead of killing her with us, it's better to leave her with Mia to live her life without threat." My mom and Uncle George started to cry and accepted Abigail's point, but my heart refused to accept it. They convinced me to leave Olivia with Mia.

With a heavy heart, I left my daughter with Mia in the New Cloud Town. I kissed my daughter many times with tears and gave three-fourths of my money to Mia to take care of my daughter. We left Uncle George with Mia as support, but not permanently. After arranging everything with Mia and Olivia, Uncle George would come to us.

With tears, Abe and I left Olivia with Mia in New Cloud Town. Then we reached West Coast Town and built a house. After two months, Uncle George came to us.

CHAPTER TWENTY-THREE

NEW LIFE

On the 30th of July 1933, Uncle George visited us in the West Coast town, which was 2000 km away from New Cloud town and nearly 4000 km away from Moonshine town. When Uncle George arrived, we had already built a beautiful new house and a restaurant next to it. He was pleased to see the two buildings, and we named the restaurant HOLIGIRL Restaurant. Uncle George, Abe, and my mom were the chefs at the restaurant, but I did not know how to cook. They taught me many recipes and made me one of the chefs at the restaurant. Our restaurant became popular among the people of the West Coast town and began to earn more. However, we felt an emptiness in our hearts as we missed Olivia. We decided not to disturb Olivia and Mia, fearing we might bring trouble to them.

Days passed, and it was August 1934. We had become very famous in the West Coast town, and life was returning to normal. One day, Abe woke me up and told me she was pregnant. I was overjoyed and kissed her forehead, but she did not seem happy. I asked her why she looked worried instead of smiling brightly. She replied, "After he is born, we will have to give him up to someone else. My babies are not mine." She left the room sadly. I threw the blanket off and ran after her. I took her hand and said, "Today, I am going to bring her back. Is that okay with you, my dear pregnant lady?" I laughed and hugged her. She kissed me and jumped like a deer. She helped me pack. After finishing the packing of the luggage, Abe and I went to my mom and Uncle George. Then she told them about our pregnancy. They were also very happy to know that. I told them about my journey to bring my daughter Olivia to us. It was a memorable day, August 12, 1934, which also happened to be my mom's birthday. After lunch, they sent me off with joy and the expectation of seeing Olivia. I reached the railway station and boarded the train to New Cloud Town. After 2 days, I arrived at New Cloud Town.

In New Cloud Town, I had breakfast at a nearby restaurant. The town was well developed compared to two years ago. After finishing my breakfast, I walked to the location where I had left my daughter. It was completely changed. I was a little nervous to see my daughter. When I reached the spot, I was confused to see a mansion. I was clueless and asked the neighbors about them, but they didn't know anything. However, I saw an old man in a shop near that mansion whom I had seen the day I left my daughter. I inquired about them. He said, "Yeah, I know you and those two girls. They are very good and genuine people, but they left this place a year ago. They sold this house to someone, and now it has been changed into a mansion." I was speechless, and my entire dream was shattered. The old man gave me a letter that Mia had written. In that letter, she wrote:

Dear Brother Ethan,

You gave me a new life, and then you gave me your life. Uncle George helped us build the house, but I saw some cops in the hunt for you and Olivia, so I left New Cloud

Town. Don't worry, Ethan. Olivia will be safe with me. It's a promise. I will raise her as a good citizen. I also changed her name, Ethan, because the cops got her name but I don't know how they knew it. I promise you that I won't die without telling you our address. When she reaches 28, we will come back to Moonshine. Please convey this to my sister, Abigail. The moment you left her to me, I started to breastfeed her. Olivia looks like her and acts like you, Ethan. I will take care of her as my daughter, and she also calls me mamma. Twice a year, I try to post letters anonymously. Let's meet after 26 years, Ethan.

With love,

Mia.

I was shocked because I didn't know how my daughter would be raised in her hands. However, I gained trust in her and left the place with great grief. I was worried about going back home without my daughter. I was very saddened for her mother, who had high expectations that were shattered when I saw her. Even while traveling, I didn't sleep at all due to my sorrow. Upon reaching home, I explained everything to Abe, my mom, and Uncle George. My mom and Uncle George accepted and understood the situation, but Abe did not. I understood her feelings as a mother. Later, she also understood the situation, and we lived a happy life. Doctors and Abe informed me that she was carrying twins, which brought happiness not only to me but to my family as well. Abe gave birth to twins, a boy and a girl, and we continued to live a joyful life.

On April 24, 1947, Uncle George passed away at the age of 75. On October 7, 1953, my mom died of a heart attack. My son and daughter excelled in their studies at top universities. Our restaurant business continued to run smoothly. We shared our past experiences with our children, who were very supportive. They got married to their loved ones and settled in foreign countries. They asked us to join them, but we declined. In April 1960, we sold our restaurant and all our possessions in the West Coast town and returned to Moonshine. We bought a small house in Moonshine. We came to Moonshine in the hope of seeing our daughter, Olivia, on her birthday.

Although we have both grown old, our love for each other has not diminished. She still looks beautiful and sexy, with her tempting lips and hips. We have enjoyed every moment of our lives, and have matured to the point of accepting everything.

On May 14, 1960, we received a letter from Mia stating that she would be waiting for us on May 16th in the place where Uncle George's restaurant used to be. As she had promised, she was there waiting for us. When we saw her, we ran to hug her with tears in our eyes.

We then went to a nearby restaurant and reminisced about our past. Mia informed us that Olivia would be celebrating her 28th birthday at the Icon Cafe at 8:00 p.m. She asked us to meet her there. Following her instructions, we went to the cafe and anxiously waited for Olivia's arrival. When Mia gestured that Olivia would arrive soon, we felt tense and nervous.

Olivia eventually arrived at the cafe, looking like a younger version of Abe. Both Abe and I were in tears at the sight of her. She looked gorgeous. We watched Olivia throughout the party, and at the end, she gave the cake to everyone in the cafe, including us. We blessed her. Mia promised to keep us informed of Olivia's daily whereabouts. We followed her discreetly everywhere she went, except for the motel where she went with her boyfriend. However, we had stopped following her for the past week as Abe had fallen ill.

Abigail was my backbone. She was a very strong person, my support. She was very open-minded and accepted reality easily. When she fell ill, she smiled and said, "Darling, I know that I won't make it. I will only live for a few more days. I have lived my entire life fully and enjoyed every second of it with you. You are my soul. I will leave you fulfilled, my love. You are my God, Ethan." I shed tears, but she told me not to cry and to accept it. Whenever I gave her medicine, she would smile sarcastically. I spent all my energy taking care of her, but yesterday she left me while sleeping in my arms.

My life ended there. The moment my Abe left me, my soul left my body and followed her. I buried her in my backyard. I couldn't find any purpose in my life, so I surrendered myself to the police.

Epilogue

Everyone on the floor was in silence as they keenly listened to my story without minding their work. Richard, the reporter, was very happy because he had content for his news channel. He thanked me for the information and then asked about my twin children, but I replied, "Sorry, kid. I can't tell you that." He begged me for the name, but I refused to disclose it. He then asked about Sam, Danny, and Aunt Sandra, but I refused to answer it too.

Richard didn't stop his questioning, but Angelina opened the cell and asked him to leave the police station. She said, "We have business with Ethan, so could you please move your ass out of here?" In fear, Richard gathered his gear and equipment and left the floor. Angelina was tense and shouted, "It's already 4:45 p.m., guys. Get ready and gear up." She helped me stand, knowing that they were going to hand me over to the escort team. I asked Angelina for two minutes to talk to everyone on the floor. She checked the time and allowed me to proceed. I said, "Thank you to all the men and women on this floor. I know it may seem ridiculous to thank the cops for arresting me, but thank you. I know you will dig up my love's grave again, but I have a request. Please bury me in the same pit where Abe was buried. I am okay with being buried next to my love in my backyard or a new grave, but please bury me with her. In my pants' pocket, I have a letter with the address of my home and one more thing. I don't want to live my remaining life. So please act accordingly."

Everyone on the floor showed empathy towards me, including Angelina. After a few minutes, the intercom rang and Angelina picked it up. She put the phone back and said, "Okay," then she shouted, "The escort team has arrived at our station. They are waiting in the parking lot. Bring Ethan to the parking lot." As soon as she announced that, everyone on the floor formed a pattern, leaving me in the center. Angelina was behind me, and Harrison Ford was in front of me.

Angelina shouted, "Move," and everyone started walking towards the parking lot. I knew Harrison was carrying a gun in his right-side holster. When we reached the parking lot, there were more than 50 special force officers with armor and machine guns. I said, "I love you, Abe. I am coming," in a low voice that made Harrison turn around. Seizing the moment, I took the gun from Harrison's holster and turned back to Angelina. I aimed the gun at my head and said, "Bye, sweetheart."

[Gunshot]